Takeover

Takeover

Jack Spangenberger

My Book Shepherd

EVANSTON, ILLINOIS

ISBN 978-1-981-64347-9

Library of Congress Control Number 2018901501

Project management by Carlyle Carter

Book design and composition by Karen Sheets de Gracia
in the Tisa and Astounder typefaces

Cover illustration by Jay Montgomery

Printed by CreateSpace

For Sharon

and for

Evelynn, Ryan, and Abby

ACKNOWLEDGMENTS

The idea for this story was born in the mid-1980s, when I first started writing it. There were many pauses (sometimes quite lengthy) because of life's various interruptions. Over time, hundreds of friends, acquaintances, and one special editor and coach encouraged and guided me with ideas and critiques. Here is a mention of those who helped me along the way.

Over many years, my fourth- and fifth-grade students in Wilmette, IL, listened and contributed ideas for the story and convinced me that the novel was a worthy endeavor. Sharon Holt, my wife and main support, who is a first-grade teacher, shared her gifted insights, suggestions, and support throughout the long process of writing and publishing this novel. Carlyle Carter, my editor, guided me through the stages of editing and publishing this book. Her editorial skills, encouragement, and patience directed and took me on a literary journey much richer than anything I ever experienced before. Cindy Morgan was my great helper and my faithful and extremely patient guide with editing and technology during the long writing process.

Linda Garcia, a third-grade teacher and friend, gave me important insights and ideas. Theresa Oakes, also a good friend, read the manuscript to her fifth-grade class of 2006–07 at Smith School in Danvers, MA, and related their suggestions to me. Judy Kiss and Fiona Bailey, kindergarten teachers, helped me with insights into six-year-olds and allowed me to observe their classrooms.

Jill Gontovick, a fifth-grade teacher, critiqued the manuscript. Sixth grader Ben Butler of Evanston, IL; fifth grader Sarah Betker of Elmhurst, IL; and fourth grader and fantastic godson Dylan Turner of Highland Park, IL, offered valuable comments to improve the story. Keira Nilson, fifth grader and totally awesome niece, gave me great encouragement to publish *Takeover*. She even submitted a book report about it. Jeff Spangenberger, my adult son with good kid-insight, critiqued the manuscript. Lucy Bruzas, former librarian at Jackson School, Elmhurst, IL; Marlene Tar Brill; and Jamie Gilson offered me sound and experienced publishing advice. My friend Bob Turner was a good sounding board over the years.

Greg Pietka, a retired drafting teacher at Lane Technical High School, did the school layout.

I am eternally grateful to all of those mentioned. It has been a special and fulfilling experience to share with all of you.

CONTENTS

Central School

1995

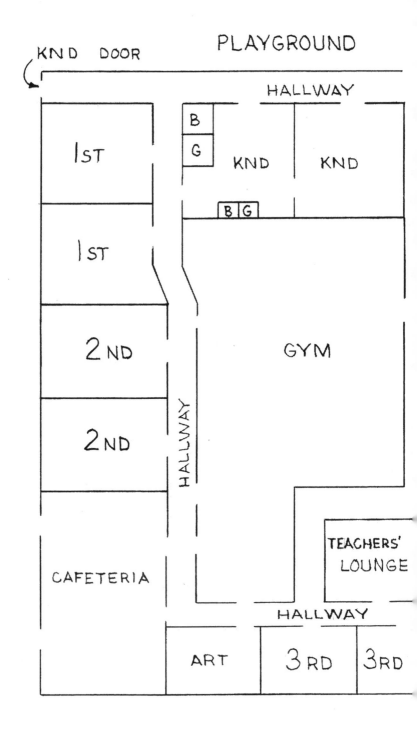

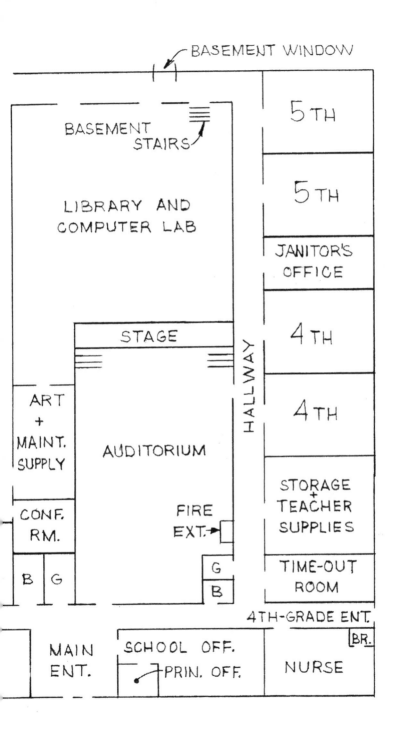

He Wiggled Like a Fish

Mr. Alston was sitting in his reclining chair when the phone rang. The Thursday evening newspaper he was reading was flat on his lap. His living room clock showed eight thirty when he reached for his phone.

"Hello!"

"Hello, Mr. Alston?"

"Yes!"

"This is Sal Maglie from our town water department. There's been a water main break in the back of Central School. One of the neighbors reported seeing water on the playground."

"What?"

"It's nothing to be alarmed about. There's a crew over there working on it now, but we won't be able to get water service into the school until late tomorrow.

Mr. Alston didn't recognize the man's voice. He said, "Uh oh! We can't have school without water. I'll have to call the school superintendent. We'll be right over."

"That isn't necessary, Sir. We have already called the superintendent. I caught her at a very busy time, and she asked me to call you. She wants you to phone the teachers and other staff that work at the school. You don't have to worry about notifying the students. She said she would alert the parents tonight through a telephone and e-mail network that the PTA uses. And there's no need for you to be here. It's a pretty messy job, and we'd rather have just our own people here. The superintendent told me to tell you to just take the day off."

"Really? You don't need me to get into the school or anything?"

"Nope! We have already gotten a key."

"Well, all right. I'll notify the school staff."

Mr. Alston was already thinking about what he might do with his extra day off. "If you need me for anything just give me a call. I can be there in ten minutes."

"I sure will, Mr. Alston. This is a routine job for us. We'll be finished before dinnertime tomorrow. The school will be good as new when the doors open again on Monday. Enjoy your day off, Sir."

"Well, thank you, Mr. Maglie. I think I will."

Mr. Alston hung up and called to his wife in the next room. "Hey, Honey, school's been called off tomorrow; water main break."

"Oh!" she answered. "Great, Dear. You have just gotten a surprise three-day weekend. Congratulations."

"Thank you." He picked up the newspaper and continued reading.

* * *

At seven forty-five on Friday, the next morning, Phil Rizzuto was as nervous as a Little League kid at bat with two outs and the bases loaded. He stood at the bottom of the stairs with his jacket and backpack already on. He hoped his voice wouldn't betray his excitement when he called up to his parents in their bedroom. "Bye, Mom and Dad!" He scrunched his face, hoping to hear them say good-bye. His mother yelled from her bedroom. "You're leaving now? It's not even eight o'clock!"

"I know, but my teacher said she would help me with some math if I came in early. I already ate. I'd better get going. Bye!" he yelled. He wanted to cut out any conversation so he started for the door.

"Okay, Phil, have a good day!" his mother answered.

"Bye, Phil," yelled his dad.

He shot out the front door, leaving his parents staring at each other. They wondered if this was the age when kids began to take their schoolwork seriously.

Six minutes later he was at the school, standing by the back window. It looked like the window of a jail because of the three bars on its front. Phil was not visible from the street. He wore sweatpants and a navy blue jacket that zipped up the front. They were the darkest clothes he could find. He looked around for witnesses.

"Good, no one there."

He knelt on the blacktop in front of the window and reached through the bars. He pushed hard on the window's wooden frame. The hinges squeaked a complaint as the window swung wide open.

Phil forced his backpack through the bars, and barely heard it hit the basement floor. Next he took off his jacket, balled it up, and shoved it through. He lay down on his side, and feet-first he wiggled like a fish, sliding his body between two of the bars. With much effort he pulled with his hands and forced his hips through.

Phil had a sudden horrifying thought. What if someone had spotted him and was making a phone call? In minutes the police would be there, grabbing him by his hair before he made it through.

He moved even faster until his legs dangled down into the room, and his body twisted. He worked his head through. Finally, hanging by his hands, with his back to the room, he let go and dropped to the floor.

"Thump!"

He stumbled backward and nearly tripped over his jacket. "Phew! I'm in!"

He turned and looked around the dark room. Only a little light came through the barred window. It was enough for him to see a broom leaning against the wall and piles of dusty textbooks on a broken desk. There was a plastic bowl from the art room with its insides covered in dry paint. The room was quiet and smelled dusty.

"I gotta get moving," he whispered to himself. He grabbed the broom and used it to push the window back to its usual position. He swiped up his jacket and backpack and rushed toward the stairway.

As he climbed the dark stairs, he looked up and saw a line of morning light squeezing under the bottom of the door. He knew that this door was never locked. He grabbed the knob, turned it, and opened the door.

"Yes!" he exclaimed. He entered the fourth- and fifth-grade hallway and stopped to listen. It was strangely quiet. He felt like a spy in enemy headquarters. Phil hurried down the hallway, passing rooms he had never seen empty before. At the far end of the hallway near the washroom he stopped at the fourth-grade entrance. None of his buddies were there yet.

"Good!" he said.

It was a little after eight o'clock. He jogged to his locker, hung up his jacket and backpack, and rushed back to the door. He leaned against the wall, gave a sigh of relief, and waited for his partners in crime.

Classroom Preparation

Phil pushed as hard as he could to open the school door. "Hurry up," he hissed. Dusty Rhodes and Gil Hodges burst through the entrance and into the hallway. Phil poked his head out into the October morning and scanned the neighborhood.

"Good, no one watching."

He yanked the door closed. For a moment the three of them stared at one another. Dusty spoke first. "I can't believe this! We are actually doing it." He turned to Phil. "Any problems getting in?"

Phil smiled. "No! It was easy."

"Okay! It's 8:10," Gil stated. "We've got forty minutes before the first bell. Phil, you stay here and let everyone in. C'mon Dusty." Gil and Dusty hurried down the hallway. When they got to the school office, Gil said, "I'll meet you here and give you the key." Dusty nodded and continued on past the office. His first job was to turn on all the hallway lights. Gil unlocked the office door and went in.

Meanwhile, Phil pushed open the school door again to let in Sadie Harding and Priscilla Wright. He jerked it closed as they rushed by him. "Who's here?" Priscilla whispered.

Phil kept his voice calm. "Gil, Dusty, and me are the only ones so far. Everything's cool. You're supposed to go to your rooms and get ready."

"Okay!" they said. The girls scooted down the hallway and disappeared.

Dusty returned to the office as Gil was looking through a ring of keys he got from the secretary's desk. Dusty asked, "Is that where you found the master key?"

"Yeah," Gil answered. "It was right on top of these paper clips." He pointed into the open drawer.

Dusty was wearing a new pair of suspenders. He was the only kid in school who wore suspenders. He told his friends his grandpa wore suspenders, and when he talked about him he always said, "My grandpa is the best grandpa in the world." He had collected six pairs of suspenders since first grade, and all of them were bright red.

Gil handed the master key to him and said, "Okay, you know the plan. Open all the classrooms and offices." Dusty nodded and shot out of the office and toward the third-grade rooms. Gil unlocked the principal's office and switched on the ceiling light. He placed a pad of paper and a pencil in the center of the glass-top desk and sat down in the chair. He leaned back, placed his arms on the armrests, and stretched out his legs. He rocked and swiveled and interlocked his fingers, placing his hands on his lap.

"Dad should see me now," he thought.

Phil still waited at the fourth-grade hallway entrance door, watching for more classmates. "I've got the best job of all. I break in. I let everyone in. I get to be gym teacher. I could be famous when this is all over," he imagined.

Loud knocking snapped him back to reality. There were Whitey Lockman and Bobby Thompson staring with huge eyes through the glass. He pushed the door open. Whitey and Bobby almost knocked him down as they rushed in. They acted like someone was chasing them.

Whitey asked Phil, "Everything okay?"

Bobby asked, "Is Gil here yet?"

"Yeah," answered Phil, trying to sound like he was in charge. "Gil's here. So's Dusty. You better get going." Bobby nodded and trotted off to his classroom, and Whitey headed for the janitor's office.

Next to arrive were Leo Durocher and Sarah Glum. Once inside the door Leo spoke in an excited whisper. "This is better than when we snuck into the girl's bathroom!"

Sarah glared at him. "Gross!" she cried out.

"Let's go!" said Leo. He headed for the nurse's office, and Sarah hurried to her second-grade classroom.

After standing at the door for twenty minutes Phil hurried to the office. "Everyone is here! It's all going as planned. This is awesome."

"Yeah, Phil, so far so good." said Gil. He opened a desk drawer and grabbed a piece of metal that looked like a bent pencil. "Here's the Allen wrench. Unlock all the student entrance doors at 8:40. Okay?"

Phil held the wrench up and said, "Yup! This is all I need. I'll lock them all up again at 9:05."

Gil said, "Don't forget to unlock the fourth-grade entrance at lunch recess."

"Right," answered Phil.

Gil had the principal's office organized and ready for the day. His father had taught Gil that organizing and planning were necessary to "achieve, lead, and succeed." That was his father's favorite topic of conversation. His dad coached him on how to "work people." He said things like, "Watch those around you and figure out what's important to them, notice what their habits are. Listen to what they say, show interest in them, look them in the eye, and react like what they're saying is important. Never yell; never lose control of yourself. That's how you lead." Sometimes Gil felt like he was an employee of his dad rather than his son.

Dusty sat down at the secretary's desk. His role for the day was to deal with the unexpected. He would take phone calls and watch the monitor that showed the front-door entrance. He was in charge of watching for any visitors. His job was to push the button that unlocked the front door to allow them in.

Leo was in the nurse's office, right next to the main office. He knew that the nurse went to the cafeteria every day and took ice cubes from the freezer to fill up her small bucket. She used the ice for most of the students' complaints. He made sure the ice bucket was full.

Gil saw that the office was ready for the day. "Dusty, I'm going to check the rooms."

"Okay! Me and Leo will stay here."

Gil walked out and past the teachers' lounge, down the south hallway, looking into the third-grade and art rooms. He was hunting for anything that might cause a problem. Any mistake could blow the whole operation. He was looking to see that the "teachers" were in the classrooms and setting up for the day. He was glad the building had only one floor and only two classrooms for each grade. Anything bigger would have been too much to handle.

He continued around to the other side of the building. He looked at the first- and second-grade rooms, then the kindergarten area. He was pleased to see that all the "teachers" were in their rooms setting out papers, writing instructions on whiteboards, putting chairs in proper positions, and turning on computers. His next stop was the gym. Gil found Phil in the equipment room. He had a whistle hanging around his neck, and he was lining up the kick balls. Phil looked at his watch and said, "I'm almost ready for class. In a couple of minutes I'll unlock the three main doors."

It was 8:40. Gil reminded him to relock the doors after classes started. As he left, Phil called after him, "I am totally psyched, Gil. This is going to be an awesome day." Gil flashed the thumbs-up sign as he left to visit the fourth- and fifth-grade hallway. At the janitor's office, he saw Whitey moving some tools around. Gil stepped in and saw that the brooms, rags, and a bucket were neatly lined up against the wall. Whitey turned to

Gil and exclaimed, "This place was a mess. I'm cleaning it up a little."

Gil laughed. "It looks really good, Whitey. I'm sure Mr. Winter will appreciate it. The bell is going to ring soon. I just checked the rooms and everyone is ready." As he turned to go, the two boys shared huge smiles.

His final inspection stop was the nurse's office. He said to Leo. "All set?" The ice bucket and bandages were lined up and ready for the day.

Leo nodded his head and grinned, "Ready to go!"

Dusty was still at the secretary's desk when Gil returned. He watched his friend snap a suspender against his shirt with his thumb, something he did when he was excited. Gil was excited too. "Just a few more minutes and the doors open, Dusty. We're going to do this. We'll show them." Dusty smiled back at his friend and snapped again.

Both boys looked up at the clock with the automatic timer. It was the clock that triggered the bell to ring at exactly 8:50. Through the office window they saw the usual crowd of students outside, standing around, talking, and waiting.

"It's 8:48!" Dusty exclaimed, "Well, here we go. Good luck to us!" *Snap.*

Gil answered, "Dusty, trust me! This is going to work!"

The bell sounded at 8:50. The students waiting outside quickly began to surge forward toward the main entrance as they did every morning. The two boys watched through the office door window as students, talking loudly to one another, pressed through the front door and hurried toward their rooms. Their movement through the hallway made Dusty think of flowing lava. Gil spoke to Dusty quietly, almost like a prayer. "They have no idea that they will remember this day for the rest of their lives."

The takeover had begun.

Carl Furillo and
Mrs. Dower

Nine days earlier, during a Wednesday morning recess, Carl Furillo charged into Gil on the grassy schoolyard. Gil saw him coming at the last second, but it was too late to react. Carl's first punch grazed off Gil's shoulder, but the next one caught him right on his ear. He fell backwards a few steps, and Carl came after him again. Gil grabbed Carl's arms, and the two boys twisted and grunted until they crashed to the ground. The other students quickly gathered to watch.

Gil and Carl ended up with their arms and legs locked together. Neither one wanted to give up his grip. Carl was snarling, " . . . tired of you telling me what to do! You think you're the big shot around here." His face was as red as a cherry.

Gil was breathing hard and holding on. His hair was messed up, and his ear was starting to swell. He stared down at the grass, thinking about his next move. After a few seconds he said, "I'm going to let go now, Carl. Just cool it."

Carl didn't move. Gil eased his hold, and they carefully began to untangle. Carl's face was pinched in anger.

Both boys stood up and faced each other, watching to see what the other would do next. Gil backed away and said, "C'mon, Carl. Don't be such a jerk! I don't want to get in trouble."

Carl answered back, "You won't if you just mind your own business. You are not nearly as cool as you think you are."

"Whatever!" said Gil as he turned to walk away. The crowd began to break up.

Mrs. Dower was the teacher supervising recess that day. She was the meanest teacher at Central School and maybe in the whole state. She liked being mean. Her face always looked like she was straining to lift a heavy weight. No one at school ever saw her smile. She always had tension lines around her eyes. Her black hair was pulled back tightly into a bun, which made her forehead look like a shiny, overinflated balloon.

Earlier that morning she had scolded a kindergarten girl for walking too quickly in the hallway. When the child began crying, Mrs. Dower said, "Stop that crying or I'll give you something to cry about." The little girl's breathing became jerky as she tried to calm herself. Mrs. Dower snapped, "Now, get to your room!" She stared as the girl waddled down the hallway.

When Gil and Carl were fighting, Mrs. Dower looked across the long, blacktopped playground and spotted a group of fifth graders grouped together. Scowling, she walked toward them, muttering to herself, "Somebody is up to no good over there!" She caught a glimpse of two boys releasing their holds on each other.

When Gil walked away from Carl, he suddenly felt Mrs. Dower's tight grip on his arm. "Stop right there, you!" she barked. She yelled at Carl, "Over here, young man! Now!" She curled her index finger at him. The onlookers had moved away, glancing sideways to watch what would happen next. Mrs. Dower waved her free arm at them. "Go away, people! Mind your own business!" They all turned their heads and wandered off in different directions.

Carl glared at Gil as Mrs. Dower began, "Now, you two were fighting, and I won't have that kind of behavior in this school. You settle your differences some other way."

Gil thought, "You should talk! You never settled anything without screaming and yelling."

She continued, "I don't know what happened or who started it, and I don't care. I want the two of you in my classroom right after school today. I'm going to teach you not to misbehave at recess, and that will include a letter to your parents about what just happened." She waved her hand over her head and said, "Now get away from me! I don't want to be near you!"

At that moment the bell rang and 250 Central School pupils ran toward the school, squeezed through the entrance doorways, and walked down the hallways to their classrooms.

Gil's ear throbbed.

Becky and Hank

Gil woke up the next morning with a worried feeling. It wasn't because of Mrs. Dower's letter. His mom wasn't too upset about that because she knew Mrs. Dower usually made a big deal over nothing. He was worried because having Carl around was like having a small, irritating pebble in his shoe. He didn't want to get into any fights, especially with that hothead. Carl was always looking out for himself and didn't care about anybody else. He exploded like a volcano when he got mad.

While getting dressed, Gil thought about how he liked school a lot, mainly because he could be with his friends. Today he felt lazy, however; he just wanted to stay home and do nothing. It was a feeling he had when he was bothered about something.

A little later he sat at the kitchen table finishing a bowl of cereal. His little sister, Becky, sat in her high chair. "Peek-a-boo!" she screamed. Gil glanced up and saw his baby sister peeking at him through her fingers.

"Peek-a-boo!" he answered. Becky squealed a really loud laugh. "Hey," he said, "your pajamas are soaked with milk! Where's your bib?" She pointed to the floor and frowned. Her chin was wet with milk. "Yuck," he said.

"Peek-a-boo!" she repeated. Gil changed the game.

He made a different funny face every time she peek-a-booed him.

Becky shouted, *"Eeeeek! Aaaah!"* each time. Then he made his best face. He pushed his left cheek up and his right cheek down with his hands, crossed his eyes, stuck out his tongue, and flapped his lips. Becky shouted in glee as she kicked her feet and waved her hands over her head.

"Gotta go, Becky. Don't wanna be late for school."

As he got up, he puffed out his cheeks and made his eyes as round as he could. She laughed again when he walked over to pick up his backpack. He yelled good-bye up the stairs to his parents and then started for the door. He turned to blow Becky a kiss, and when he saw her he cried, "Oh no! Becky! What did you do?"

She had picked up her bowl of soggy cereal and dumped it over her head. She giggled as the mess slid down her pajama top. Some of it rested on her lap, and some slipped farther down, inside her loose diaper.

"What a mess!"

She laughed again.

"Becky, you don't put cereal on your head!" He tried to sound strict. She stuck out her tongue and blew at him. She rubbed the mushy cereal into her soggy pajama top with both hands. Gil grabbed a paper towel and wiped her face.

"No!" she squealed and pushed his hand away.

"Let me clean you up," he said sharply. Becky squealed again as she put the bowl back on top of her head. Gil grabbed it and put it in the sink. Then she screeched so loud that her parents, who were upstairs, heard her.

"Hey, what's going on down there?" his mother asked as she started down the stairs. At the same time, the phone rang.

"I'll get it," he said. It was his chance to avoid his mother when she saw the mess.

"Hello?" he answered.

"What on earth! Becky!" cried their mother.

Dusty, Gil's best friend, said. "Hi, Gil. Meet you at the corner in a minute?"

Gil could see his mom picking bits of cereal out of Becky's hair. She looked at Gil and slowly shook her head. Becky pouted.

"Hang on a second, Dusty. Mom, she dumped the bowl over her head." He waited a moment and said, "It's Dusty. Can I walk with him?"

"Yes, Gil, go ahead. I'll just throw her in the tub."

Mr. Hodges suddenly appeared in the kitchen, dressed as usual in a business suit. He looked at Becky, then at Gil. Becky stared at her father like she was expecting a scolding.

"What happened?" he said sharply.

When Gil finished explaining, his dad said, "I'll bet if you were watching her you could have stopped her." His dad shook his head with an impatient look.

"Sorry, Dad."

Mr. Hodges kissed his wife quickly on the cheek, said good-bye, and walked out the door.

Gil looked at his mom. "Go ahead," she said.

"Okay, Dusty," he said quietly. "I'll be right there."

Becky picked off a piece of cereal from her pajama top and ate it.

* * *

Dusty was waiting at the street corner where they always met. He was watching two squirrels chase each other up and down the trunk of an oak tree. Dusty's face was thin, and his brown hair was always mussed. Dusty bellowed, "Whoa! Look at that!" One of the squirrels had leaped from a tree branch to a branch in another tree. The second squirrel followed right after, and the race continued. "That's so cool!" he exclaimed as he snapped a suspender.

Gil added, "They are fun to watch sometimes. My dad says that squirrels are nothing more than rats with fluffy tails."

"Oh, I never thought of that. Squirrels are rodents, but they're so cute."

"I know," said Gil, "but if they get in your house they can be dangerous."

"You sound like your dad," said Dusty. "Why is he always so serious? Remember that twenty-minute lecture on not wasting money?"

"I know," answered Gil, "but he's fun sometimes. He's trying to teach me good habits."

"I'd like to see him teach you about fun."

"Let's go," said Gil.

As they began walking, Gil sighed, "I wish we didn't have to go to school today. I don't feel like sitting there for six hours."

"Me neither!" responded Dusty. "Except for Science. I think I'm going to like today's experiment." They were studying motion, and Mrs. Garcia was teaching them about force. She said that in the seventeenth century, a math genius from England named Isaac Newton stated that a force in one direction has an equal force in the opposite direction. She gave the example that when a person is stepping from a small boat onto a dock, he exerts a force on the boat in order to go toward the dock. The boat is pushed in the opposite direction. Dusty liked talking about stuff like that.

"I want to see the milk-carton experiment," Dusty said. Mrs. Garcia promised the class a demonstration on how to use a one-gallon milk carton as a rocket. She said they would be using rocket fuel, which she would actually ignite to shoot the carton across the room.

"Yeah, I like the science experiments," replied Gil, "but today I'm feeling blah, as my mom puts it. No energy."

Dusty laughed. "Remember in third grade when Duke used baking soda instead of baby powder in that chemistry experiment? The room smelled like vinegar for a week."

"Yeah!" chuckled Gil. "Mr. Wilkins didn't laugh though, and he never found out who switched the labels on the bottles."

A motorcycle roared by the two boys as they walked. The rider wore dark sunglasses, blue jeans with holes, and a loose shirt.

"There's that guy," said Dusty. "I see him walking around our school when he's not on his hot motorcycle. He lives in your neighborhood."

"Yeah," replied Gil. "He's okay."

"I think he's weird."

"I know. He looks tough, but he's not a bad guy."

* * *

Gil thought back to last summer when he saw the guy working on his motorcycle behind his house. Their yards backed up to each other. He had seen him riding around the neighborhood for a long time, and he decided to walk over to check out the gleaming motorcycle.

Gil greeted him shyly, "Hi."

"Hi," the guy replied.

"Is that your motorcycle?"

"Yeah," answered the guy.

"What are you working on?"

"Puttin' in a new fuel line." He never looked up at Gil, just kept working on his shiny engine.

"Oh! You a mechanic?"

"No, I just know a lot about motors."

"Oh. That's a real nice motorcycle," said Gil.

"Thanks."

The guy had lived there for years, but the two had never spoken before. He looked like he was about twenty years old. Gil's parents told him not to get too friendly with him.

Gil asked, "What's your name?"

"Hank."

"Mine's Gil. I live in that house." Gil turned his head and jerked a thumb over his shoulder.

Hank looked up at the house, then back at the wrench he was turning.

"I'm not very good at fixing things," said Gil. "I usually give up after a while."

"Yeah," said Hank. He kept on working.

Gil asked, "Do you want to be a mechanic?"

Hank said, "That's the only thing I ever wanted to be."

"I bet you'd be good. You look like you know what you're doing."

"Thanks."

"I go to Central School," said Gil.

"I thought so. I've seen you walking there. I went to Central too, a long time ago." Hank glanced up quickly at Gil.

"So, when do you get to be a mechanic?"

Hank shifted his body to face Gil. "Well, it's a little complicated. I could learn at Tom's Cycle Shop here in town, but that doesn't seem to be working. I got into a little trouble and word got around. People don't want me working in their stores. They're afraid I'll steal something. I could also go to motorcycle mechanics school over in Maplewood, but that costs money."

"Oh! How much?" asked Gil.

"It costs $1,500, but it might as well be $8,000, because I'm broke."

"What about your parents helping you out?"

"They don't like motorcycles."

Gil asked, "Can't you save for it?"

"I tried that, but the jobs I got didn't last long. Something always happened, and I got fired. Those bosses were snippy if I was a little late, and sometimes I argued with the customers. They liked my work, but they didn't like the other stuff."

"Too bad."

"I'm workin' on it though. I told 'em I'd try to be nicer and be on time, but they don't want to take a chance on me."

"I guess that motorcycle school would be the best thing for you to do," said Gil.

"I talked to the mechanic about the class. He said with my experience, I could take the short course at a lower cost and get certified sooner; but it still costs $1,500 with $900 down and $600 due in six months."

"Whoa, that's a lot of money, Hank. I sure hope you can do it someday."

"Yeah, thanks."

Gil said, "Well, I gotta go, and I really like your motorcycle. See you around, okay?"

"Sure, so long kid."

* * *

Gil and Dusty crossed the street near the school. "Mornin' boys!" said the crossing guard.

"Good morning, Mrs. Cavannah!" She stood in the middle of the intersection and held up the red stop sign even though there were no cars coming. Gil and Dusty walked slowly to the wide concrete area near the front door of the school. They stood outside with other students, waiting for the 8:50 A.M. bell. It was 8:35 A.M. While they were waiting, Gil told Dusty about the cereal bowl Becky had spilled over her head.

"Did your dad get mad?"

"Not too bad," answered Gil. "He grumbled a little; then he left for work."

"Good," said Dusty.

Gil chuckled, "I'm glad I have a baby sister."

* * *

When the bell rang, the students crammed through the main doorway and made their way to their classrooms. Mrs. Garcia was at her desk grading papers. "Good morning, Dusty! Good morning, Gil!" Mrs. Garcia shot a quick look at each boy as she continued to mark papers.

The boys replied at the same time, "Good morning, Mrs. Garcia." Their desks were next to each other in the middle of the room, so they sat down and talked as the room steadily filled with students.

Suddenly Dusty yanked himself out of his chair and hustled up to Mrs. Garcia's desk. When he approached her, she looked up at him, then back down at the papers, continuing to make Xs. "Yes, Dusty?"

"Mrs. Garcia, what time do we have Science today? I've been thinking a lot about that milk-carton experiment."

She looked at him. "Oh, Dusty, I'm sorry. We have to skip Science today. We've got two Social Studies movies to see, and they have to be returned today. We'll have to wait until tomorrow to launch the rocket."

He walked back to his seat. When the bell rang, Dusty was thinking about how everything was done on a schedule: 9:05 A.M.—Reading; 9:50 A.M.—English; 10:40 A.M.—Gym; 11:20 A.M.—Lunch. Math, Science, and Social Studies were always in the afternoon. Dusty thought, "One day I want Science to last for an hour and a half."

Everyone stood up when the late-bell rang and recited the Pledge of Allegiance. Mrs. Garcia greeted her students, made an announcement about a PTA fundraiser, and reminded everyone to use the recycle baskets for papers they were discarding. "Reading assignments are on the whiteboard. I'll meet with the purple book group first. Your answers better be in complete sentences."

Gil and Dusty looked at each other. Gil faked a yawn by pumping his hand in front of his open mouth. Dusty nodded his head.

PeeWee Reese

Central School's most popular fifth-grade game was Catch One–Catch All. When morning recess began, students dashed out the school door to a huge cottonwood tree at the edge of the playground. The last one to touch the tree was "it." Anyone that the "it" person tagged joined the "it" person chasing the others. Slowly the group of "its" grew until they outnumbered the untagged. The game ended when everyone was tagged. If time allowed, they would have another round. That day Mr. Alston and Mrs. Dower were the recess supervisors. Usually the players ran in an area as far as possible from Mrs. Dower. There was no need to ask for trouble if it could be avoided.

On this morning, Sadie was "it." She wasn't the smartest student in the class, but she was really fast. The players were scattered around the entire playground, and they were watching her like field mice watch a cat.

Sadie suddenly charged a group of three girls. They screamed and bolted away in all directions. She suddenly made a sharp turn and ran full speed toward Whitey. He let her almost reach him, but then he cut to his right, leaving Sadie grabbing air. Whitey laughed. Sadie frowned.

Sadie ran to Sarah, who was standing alone at the edge of the blacktop and easily tagged her. Sarah said, "Oh, I'm not playing."

Sadie said, "Play with us today, Sarah. I could use your help."

"No," was all Sarah said in a low voice.

Sadie turned away and looked for another target. Her radar spotted Bobby. Bobby was a fun guy who liked to make people laugh. He was also standing alone, talking to himself. When Sadie got within attacking distance, he spotted her, but it was too late. Sadie caught him from behind and smacked him on the back.

Bobby moaned. "Okay," he sighed. He hated being "it," but he was ready to go after the others. Since Bobby was a pretty fast runner also, in three minutes they tagged eight more kids. All the "its" huddled together like football players. "Let's spread out and go after those three girls standing by the doorway." The "its" broke their huddle, intentionally not looking at the girls. When they felt they were close enough to their target, they sprang into a full attack.

The three girls screamed loud enough for the whole neighborhood to hear and ran in three different directions. One of them, Priscilla, charged full speed through the second-graders' game and crashed into PeeWee Reese. The little boy fell down hard on the blacktop. *"Waaa!"* he cried. He cried so loud that even kids inside the school looked out their windows to see who it was. A crowd gathered around him immediately.

"Are you okay, PeeWee?" asked a friend who knelt next to him.

PeeWee cried louder.

Priscilla never stopped running after knocking down PeeWee. She knew she had bumped someone, but she didn't see anybody go down. When she stopped and looked back, she saw a group of kids gathered around someone lying on the blacktop.

Mr. Alston and Mrs. Dower had been talking to each other and didn't see the accident. A student ran up to them and pointed toward the group, shouting, "Come quick! PeeWee just got knocked down, and he's bleeding!"

The crowd of students moved aside when the principal approached. PeeWee was lying on his back, his face wet with tears and his nose running. He had a small cut on his hand. He cried even louder when Mr. Alston squatted down next to him. Mrs. Dower spoke to the onlookers. "Go play, everybody. You don't need to gawk and stare. Go on, leave!" The students turned and slowly moved away, looking at PeeWee the whole time.

From a distance Priscilla watched Mr. Alston help PeeWee stand up. The principal said something to him, and the second grader looked around and pointed at Priscilla. Mrs. Dower fixed her eyes on Priscilla and yelled, "Priscilla Wright, you get over here right now!"

Priscilla's heart began to beat harder. "Oh no, I'm dead," she thought.

She lowered her head and walked past two fourth graders. She overheard one of them say, "I'm glad I'm not her!" When Priscilla shot her a dirty look, the girl turned away. Priscilla noticed that Sarah was watching her walk toward Mr. Alston, so she yelled at Sarah, "What are you looking at?" Sarah looked down at the ground.

Priscilla finally reached PeeWee and the principal. Mr. Alston barked, "Priscilla, I'm surprised at you, knocking down someone half your size. You didn't even stop to see if he was okay."

Mrs. Dower jumped in. "What's the matter with you?"

Mr. Alston gave Mrs. Dower an exasperated look and turned back to Priscilla. She stood there, her shoulders sagging. PeeWee had stopped crying but began snorting because he didn't have a tissue. Mr. Alston lowered his voice and scolded Priscilla, then waved her away to return to the playground. The principal took PeeWee's hand and walked him into the school. Mrs. Dower stayed outside to supervise. Her cold eyes locked onto Priscilla for almost a minute. The fifth grader walked away and didn't look back.

Gil and Dusty had observed the whole incident. As they watched Mr. Alston take PeeWee into the school, Gil said, "Something bad is going to happen. Mr. Alston was too calm. He won't let Priscilla off that easy."

Dusty snapped a suspender extra hard.

Mr. Lockman

All the students in Mrs. Garcia's classroom were watching a Social Studies movie about the Arapaho Indians when the principal entered their classroom. It was 2:30 P.M., only thirty minutes before dismissal. Mr. Alston was wearing a dark suit, white shirt, and a blue tie. His shoes were well shined. The students sat up straight in their chairs because Mr. Alston never visited a classroom unless something important was happening. He whispered into Mrs. Garcia's ear, and she nodded, clicked off the movie projector, and switched on the lights. She stood near the door, her hands folded in front of her. Priscilla sat frozen in her chair. The students were so still that their only movements were their eyes.

Mr. Alston's double chin squished outward like silly putty when he lowered his head to look at them. The ceiling lights reflected off his shiny head. "We were lucky this morning," he barked. "PeeWee wasn't hurt badly." He turned his head slowly as he eyed each student. His voice changed to low and hard as he continued, "But it could have been worse. It could have been a concussion or a broken arm. When you play a game that makes you forget about safety, I don't like that game. The game you were playing is dangerous."

Priscilla stared at her lap. Mrs. Garcia looked down at the floor. "And so," he raised his hand and pointed with his index finger, "there will be no more Catch One–Catch All on the school grounds. Ever!"

Whitey burst out, "But it was only one person's fault. Why do we all get punished? It's not fair!"

"Ever!" repeated Mr. Alston. "End of discussion!" He stomped out of the room. He didn't even look at Mrs. Garcia.

* * *

At 3:10 P.M. Dusty saw a bunch of kids talking together at the school flagpole. Sarah was standing off to the side, listening. As he walked to the pole he called to her, "Hey, Sarah, come on over to the pole with me."

"No thanks."

"Okay." He kept walking.

"Too bad about Sarah," Sadie said to Dusty when he joined his friends.

"I know," replied Dusty. "Wasn't it after third grade that she stopped playing with us? She used to joke around. All of a sudden she got shy or something. Wonder why she's hanging around today?"

Priscilla said, "Oh, just let her be. I think she's a little weird."

Sadie changed the subject. "Stoney is mean! We shouldn't all have to suffer because of what only one of us did."

"Yeah!" Leo added. "They never punish just the person who got in trouble; we all have to suffer." He turned to Priscilla. "Nothing personal, Priscilla."

"And Stoney always says it's for our own good," added Sadie. "Whitey, your father was right. Mr. Alston doesn't have a clue how to run a school." Sadie was talking about the well-known argument that Mr. Lockman and Mr. Alston had had on the playground when they were fourth graders. All the students had heard about it. It started as a polite discussion, but ended up as a shouting match. Mr. Lockman wanted to donate a huge amount of money to build a new gymnasium for the school. Mr. Alston said that those kinds of donations were gladly accepted, but the Board of Education decided how the money would be spent, not the donor.

Mr. Lockman became so angry he threw in some old complaints he had from the past, like how his son, Whitey, was being picked on by Mr. Alston and Mrs. Dower. He ended up calling the principal a stubborn fool and told him that someday everyone would find out what a lousy principal he was. Then he stomped off. Everybody knew that Mr. Lockman and Mr. Alston didn't get along.

"Yeah!" Bobby chimed in. "We're treated like babies, and they never listen to our side."

Dusty snapped both suspenders and said, "They don't trust us. They think we can't do anything, but they never let us show them we can."

Bobby said, "First they took away our bats, then they banned Frisbees, now they take away our favorite game. It's cheap!"

Whitey added, "I'd like to be in charge of the school for a while and show them how to treat kids."

"Only in your dreams!" cried Kelly. "It'll never happen. They have always controlled kids, and they always will."

Gil listened to everyone complain and agreed with his friends, although secretly he felt that Mr. Alston and his dad had a lot in common. Suddenly his face changed and his eyes widened. Whitey noticed and asked, "Gil, you look a little weird. What's the matter?"

Gil stared past everyone and said, "I've got an idea, you guys. It's crazy, but . . . ." His eyes came back into focus as he looked at his friends. "I would love to teach Stoney a lesson."

"Yeah, but how?"

Gil answered, "I don't want to say anything yet, and I don't want to look like a complete idiot. Tell you what. I'll meet you here tomorrow morning if I think my idea has a chance to work. I'll tell you about it then. C'mon, Dusty, let's go home."

The two boys walked home together, but they didn't talk. Gil thought about all the students' anger toward the principal and some of the teachers. It reminded him of a freaky conversation he had had with Whitey's dad during the summer.

* * *

He was walking by the Lockmans' mansion-like home while Mr. Lockman was watering some of his flowers.

" Hey, Gil, come on over here for a minute."

"Sure, Mr. Lockman. Your garden looks good."

"Thanks, Gil. I just wanted to tell you how impressed I have been about the way you are with your friends. I've seen you on the playground and on the baseball team. I think you're a natural leader. Really."

"Thanks, Mr. Lockman. It's probably thanks to my dad. He's always talking to me about leadership and stuff."

"That's impressive, Gil. What does he tell you?"

Gil thought for a moment. "Well, he talks about money. He tells me how to save money and how to use it for good purposes, not just for fun."

"Like, how?"

"I don't know, he tells me to save money, or to just spend it on stuff I really need, or to donate it to a good cause. He says it's good to invest in the future. Stuff like that."

"That's interesting, Gil. I want to talk to you about helping me solve a problem."

"Me?"

"Yes, you and your leadership skills."

"Okay."

"Well, you know that Mr. Alston and I don't see eye-to-eye, right?"

"Yes."

"It's really more than that. See, I think he's not a good principal for Central School. It's not just because of the way he treats Whitey. I think he's bad for the whole school . . . all you kids."

"Really?" said Gil.

"Yep! I have a long list of things he does wrong. He's been principal for over ten years, and no new programs have been added during that time. It's the same thing year after year. Even the textbooks haven't changed. Also, he doesn't think for himself. He does what the board of education members tell him to do, but they're just people who live in our town and have their own jobs during the day. They don't understand all there is to know about education. Most of us don't."

"Mr. Alston is supposed to advise the board about what's best for the school, but he waits for them to tell him what to do. He always says yes to them; he never says, 'No, here's what I think.' And the way he treats children . . . he's so quick to punish. He doesn't help a kid in trouble or show him how to do better. Have you ever seen him help a student in a kind way?"

"Well, no, not really."

Mr. Lockman asked, "Has he ever helped you out?"

"Well, I can't remember anything right now."

"Ever see him do anything special for the school?"

"Uh, no, I guess not, Mr. Lockman."

"Do you think he's a good principal, Gil?"

"I don't know. I never thought about it."

"Gil, I would want him to stay principal if he did something thoughtful; something that made the school better. I think Central School needs a person who likes children and listens to them. Also, I want a person who will make Central School special, not just ordinary. What do you think?"

"Sure, Mr. Lockman. That would be good."

"My problem is that no one will listen to me. They think I'm just mad at him and want him out, that it's a personal thing. But it isn't personal. I'm thinking of the school and all the children. Know what I mean?"

"Uh, sure, Mr. Lockman."

Mr. Lockman lowered his voice and looked around the yard. "I've been thinking about this for a long time, Gil. The board would replace Mr. Alston if anything ever happened that showed he wasn't a good principal. So, I have a proposal for you."

"Me?" asked Gil.

"Yes, you. If you ever notice anything happen that would show the community what a poor job he is doing, I would like you to think of a way to get them to see it. If you could do that, I would give you $1,000."

"Oh, Mr. Lockman, I . . . ."

"That's how strongly I feel about this, Gil. We need new leadership at Central, and nothing is going to change unless Mr. Alston improves or is replaced."

"But Mr. Lockman . . . ."

"This would be something between you and me. No one else needs to know."

"I don't think I know how to . . . ."

"Gil, remember what your dad said about saving money and not using it for fun?"

"Yes."

"This is the perfect opportunity for you. Maybe nothing will happen. I'm just saying that during your fifth-grade year, if you see something like that happen, make it so that others will know. That's all."

Gil shook his head. "Well, all right, Mr. Lockman. I doubt that I could do anything, but okay, if something happens, I'll try."

"Okay, Gil. That's fine. You are a smart kid. If nothing happens, then nothing happens, but if an opportunity arises, go for it."

"I better get going, Mr. Lockman. Thanks, uh, I'll see you."

"Sure, Gil, see you around. Hey, just between you and me."

Mr. Lockman offered his hand, and Gil shook it. "Okay, sure."

Gil never told anyone about Mr. Lockman's idea.

* * *

On their walk home from school, Dusty finally spoke up. "Seems like we're all mad at Stoney, Gil."

"Yeah."

"Too bad. I wish we had a principal we liked."

"Yep! Me too," answered Gil.

"Okay, see you tomorrow, Gil."

"See you, Dusty."

Gil's Big Idea

Gil arrived home feeling a little blue from the flagpole meeting. *"Ahhh!"* screeched Becky. She waved her arms like she was waving to friends.

"Hi, Becky!" Gil snapped out of his gloomy mood right away when he saw her. "Are you playing with your Loosey and Goosey dolls?" She picked up her two rag dolls and waved them over her head.

"Yah!" she exclaimed.

"Hi, Gil!" his mother said. She was cutting the ends off string beans at the kitchen counter.

"Hi, Mom!" He mussed Becky's hair and walked over to join his mother.

"How was school today?"

"Okay."

"Is that it? Just okay?"

"Yeah," he said flatly.

"What are you up to this afternoon?" she asked.

"I think I just want to hang around my room. I've got some homework and stuff to do."

"Okay," she said. "Dinner'll be around six."

Gil went up to his bedroom where he dropped his backpack on a chair and plopped backward onto the bed. He bounced once and clasped his hands behind his head.

He stared up at the ceiling as questions whirled in his head. "What an idea! Could it possibly work? Could it be done without getting caught? What would happen if we did get caught? Would the others be willing to do it?"

* * *

He joined his family for dinner two hours later. His mother asked, "What were you doing in your room for so long? You were very quiet."

"Oh, I had a lot of homework, and then I took it easy, just thinking."

She looked at him and sensed that he was not telling her everything. "Well, you must have a lot to think about."

At dinner Gil's parents always sat at opposite ends of the table. Gil sat on one side, and Becky sat in a highchair close to her mother on the other side. Mr. Hodges started right in. "Gil, this morning was a good example of areas where I want you to improve. In addition to organizing, I want you to think about anticipating. I'm talking about thinking ahead, watching to see what could happen. Anticipating a possible problem can prevent the problem. Do you understand what I'm talking about?"

"Yes, Dad, but it all happened so fast. One minute she was eating, and suddenly the cereal was on her head."

"I know, Gil. Those things happen, but if you get into the habit of looking ahead for problems, you can deal with them more intelligently when they happen."

"Okay, Dad. I'll remember that."

"Good," said Mr. Hodges.

* * *

Sarah quietly slipped into her house right after the flagpole meeting. She walked on tiptoes toward her room. Sarah loved her room; it was her private place. It was there that she wrote about magic kingdoms and beautiful princesses, horses, and colorful birds. Sometimes she would imagine what it would be like to be friends with Sadie and Kelly Driten.

The floor squeaked as she approached her bedroom door.

"Is that you, Sarah?"

She stopped midstep. "Yes, Mom."

"Well then, get in here!"

She plodded into the living room where her mother was watching a soap opera on television. Her mom was munching on peanut butter crackers, and she had a glass of wine next to her. "Trying to sneak in?"

"No, Mom. I was just . . . ."

"Don't lie! I know what you're thinking. You want to sit in your room and do nothing. Well, there's a lot to do, so start by cleaning up the junk you left on the table in the basement."

"It's not junk, Mom. It's the stuff I need for a play I'm writing."

"Well, you call it stuff, but I call it junk. Get it out of there."

Sarah turned toward the basement stairs as her mother grabbed a couple of crackers and turned back to the TV.

Before her dad left, her mom had been much nicer. Even though their home became more peaceful once he was gone, Sarah missed him very much and wondered if he was angry with her too. The social worker told her it wasn't her fault, but sometimes Sarah believed that it was her fault, like when he yelled at her.

Sarah cleaned up the basement table and then spent a little time in her room. At dinner she and her mother ate without speaking. The days when she and her parents laughed together, took walks, and sang songs were over. She used to love the hugs and bedtime books. Over time, though, just like a lollipop getting smaller and smaller as you lick it, those fun times happened less and were replaced by more arguing.

The day her father went off to work and never came home was when her mother's real anger began. Sarah remembers his long good-bye hug that morning. His hug gave Sarah the hope that he would come back some day.

Right after he left, her mother grumbled, "Good riddance to bad rubbish," but as the months passed she became sadder and more distant from Sarah. Her mom went to work with messy hair and wrinkled clothing, and she stopped having friends over for get-togethers. Sarah told her mother jokes and amusing stories from school to try to make her happier. She hugged her and told her she loved her. Her mother hugged her back and said, "I love you too, Sarah dear," but there was no warmth in her words. Sarah felt like her mother had wrapped up her goodness and tucked it away in some hidden place. Her goodness was replaced with sadness. Most days her mom was grumpy; some days she was even weepy. Worst of all, sometimes she ignored Sarah.

Sarah felt that she had lost both of her parents. Despite her sadness, or maybe because of it, she was determined to do well at school. Her dream was to write plays about interesting people. Happy plays. So she decided she would get involved in creative writing in high school. That goal was the engine that gave her purpose and kept her going, and she would never stop hoping her parents would get back together.

When they finished dinner, Sarah helped her mother clear the table and stack the dishes in the dishwasher. When they finished, she hugged her mom as she did each night before going to her room for the rest of the evening.

* * *

The following morning, Priscilla, Sadie, Whitey, and Bobby were waiting at the flagpole. When Gil and Dusty joined them, Priscilla spoke first. "Well, Gil, what's the big idea I heard about?"

Gil didn't hesitate. "Take over the school!" He looked at each of them.

"What do you mean by *take over*?" asked Whitey.

"I mean we take over Central School for one day. We teach the students. Just us, no grown-ups. If we plan it right, it can be done." He sounded very sure of himself.

"You're joking!" squealed Sadie.

"Are you crazy?" Priscilla asked. "Where are the teachers during all this?"

"At home," answered Gil. "They get phone calls saying the school will be closed the next day because of a plumbing problem. When they don't show up, we run the school."

"A plumbing problem?"

"Yeah. You can't run a school without water."

Priscilla cut in. "And we teach the classes?"

"Yes," answered Gil.

"You're crazy," said Sadie.

Whitey jumped in, "Well, don't you think the kindergarten and first-grade kids would get scared when they see that there are no real teachers? They'd be crying or screaming."

Gil nodded. "I think we can calm them down early on and show them that everything is going to be fine. When they start doing their regular school routine, they'll all settle down." He added, "We've been complaining about how adults are unfair and treat us like dirt. If we could pull this off, it would prove to them that we deserve more respect."

Priscilla became sarcastic. "It's an opportunity for us to get totally grounded until we graduate from high school."

Bobby added, "Or we could end up in jail."

Gil grinned, "Bobby, they don't arrest kids." He turned to Priscilla. "If we show them that we are smart enough to take charge of a whole school for a day, it will prove to them that we deserve more respect than we're getting. They'll be mad at first, but they will see what we accomplished.

"What we need to do is spread the word to fifth graders we can trust to keep a secret. Then we set up a meeting after school to talk about it. I've thought this out and I'll explain how I think we can do it. If enough of us believe it will work, we'll go ahead with the plan. If not, we'll forget it."

They stood like statues for a full half-minute. Gil said, "C'mon! At least let's meet about it." More quiet and stone faces. "Just meet with me and listen to the plan. I worked hard on it."

Dusty said, "It's scary, but I'll go to the meeting." Both suspenders snapped.

"I'm willing to talk about it," said Priscilla. Other heads nodded. Nobody wanted to be the one to chicken out.

Gil said, "Let's meet at Cameron Field today at three thirty. If you don't think it's a good idea after we talk, we'll forget about it." He pulled a folded piece of paper from his pocket. "I've already written the names of the kids I think would be good teachers and are able to keep our secret. I'll ask them to join us there. You guys shouldn't say a word to anyone."

Quiet Classroom

After their flagpole meeting, Gil and his friends filed into their classroom. Mrs. Garcia stood near her desk greeting everyone. "Good morning, Dusty, Sadie, Bobby. You all sure look alert this morning." Her greetings were usually cheery, but her students knew that once the workday began, she was all business.

"Good morning, Mrs. Garcia," they all replied. Dusty checked the day's schedule that was listed on the whiteboard. When he saw that Science was there, he looked back at Mrs. Garcia, whose eyes were on him.

"Today's the day, Dusty," she said. He smiled back.

The late bell rang. Gil looked at his watch—9:10 A.M. Mrs. Garcia presented the reading assignments to the class, but Gil's mind was not on schoolwork.

Mrs. Garcia's first reading group met with her at the round table. She called on Sadie to answer the first question. Sadie was uncomfortable. She hesitated and said, "Uh . . . ."

"Did you read the story, Sadie?"

"Well, I started it. I got halfway."

Mrs. Garcia encouraged her. "That's enough reading to answer the first question. The person that the story centers around is the main character. Who was that?"

Sadie's eyes roved around. "Uh . . . Oh sure, he was . . . uh . . . ." She shifted in her chair. "I did read, Mrs. Garcia, I just don't remember."

"Okay," replied Mrs. Garcia. "Let's find out from someone else."

"The doctor!" Carl Furillo blurted out. "Anybody could tell that. The whole story was about him."

Sadie looked down at her lap.

Mrs. Garcia's spoke angrily. "Carl, that was rude! Don't speak until I call on you. That was a terrible thing to say."

Sadie was quiet when more questions were discussed. Carl was his usual self, kicking someone's chair, throwing bits of paper. Mrs. Garcia bristled, and later, as the group returned to their seats, she motioned Carl to stay. Everyone watched. She kept her hands folded on her lap, squeezing them together as she spoke. Carl listened, then nodded as she dismissed him to his seat.

The rest of the day seemed to take forever for Gil. He looked at the clock every ten minutes. His mind wandered back to his father's talks about succeeding in life. He knew his dad loved him, but he was always lecturing him about being "the best you can be."

"When I'm a father I'm going to play with my children, take them places, crack jokes, and not be so serious all the time."

During recess, Gil talked to the people he wanted to invite to the after-school meeting. He liked the choices he had made. In the afternoon the school day seemed to move a little faster. Mrs. Garcia allowed extra time for Science. In her first experiment, she placed a small amount of "rocket fuel" into a one-gallon plastic milk carton, screwed on the cap, and shook the carton rapidly. After pouring the liquid out of the carton, she told the class, "The carton looks empty, but the vapor from the fuel is still in there. I will now lay the carton on its side on this table and place a lighted match at the opening. Watch!"

When Mrs. Garcia put a burning match to the mouth of the carton, a foot-long blue flame shot out with a loud, whooshing sound. The carton flew across the table and hit the wall. The flame died in two seconds, but the class was shocked by the noise it made and by how far it had flown. When the kids settled down, she said, "You saw the flame's force go in one direction, and the carton fly in the opposite direction. Isaac Newton knew what he was talking about."

The rest of the class was as excited as Dusty, and there was a lively discussion about rockets and engines. After a short time, Mrs. Garcia asked Dusty to demonstrate a different experiment that they had talked about earlier. Dusty stood up and showed everyone how an index card holds water inside a full glass when the glass is turned upside down. It worked well until Carl suddenly reached out and pushed the card while Dusty held the glass. The water splattered into a wastepaper basket. Dusty and Mrs. Garcia both said, "Carl!" at the same time.

Carl said, "Sorry! I couldn't resist." He gave a Mona Lisa smile.

Mrs. Garcia said, "Okay, Carl. Stay after class, please. You and I have a phone call to make."

Carl's smile changed to worry.

That was only the beginning. Bobby picked up the wet card, stuck it between his legs, and said, "Maybe this will help me hold my water. Ha ha ha."

Everyone groaned. "You're gross!" said a student. Many of them were amused though, and Bobby just smiled.

Mrs. Garcia was frustrated. "Sit down, everyone!" Bobby wasn't finished, though. He tore some paper and stuck a piece up each nostril. "No more problems with my runny nose either!" More giggles. He blew real hard through his nose, and the two papers shot down to the floor. One of them landed on Priscilla's shoe. The class laughed again, and Mrs. Garcia shouted, "Bobby! No recess on Monday. Want to try for the rest of the week?"

Priscilla looked at Bobby. "You are such a jerk," she said as she wiped off her shoe.

Gil quietly watched the whole show. He and Mrs. Garcia looked up at the clock at the same time. Only ten minutes left in the school day.

* * *

Gil stood near the picnic tables at Cameron Field. He faced the kids who showed up for the meeting and cleared his throat. "Okay, everybody, let's get started. We know how the teachers and Stoney treat us like preschoolers. Stoney just took Catch One–Catch All away from us, even though most of us were being careful. With my new idea, I think we can show the principal and the teachers that we are not babies and deserve more respect.

There were fifteen fifth graders there. Gil noticed that Sarah was among them, even though he had not invited her. Dusty was standing near her. He had always especially liked Sarah, and he wanted to show her that he supported her.

"I heard your idea, Gil," someone said. "It sounds crazy to me."

"Yeah!" came another voice. "How are we supposed to take over the school? That's impossible!"

Gil answered, "I know it sounds impossible. If you don't think it will work after I explain it to you, you don't have to do it."

"Okay, Gil, let's hear it. This oughta be good," someone else said.

Gil started. "One kid teaches each class. At Central there are only two classes in each grade, so we only need twelve classroom "teachers." We also need Art, Music, and Gym teachers, and a custodian. Also, we'll have others working in the office as the principal, secretary, and nurse."

Everyone listened quietly. When Gil finished, the questions came fast and furious.

Dusty asked, "How do we get Stoney and the teachers to *not* be there?"

Gil answered, "Does anyone here know who Sal Maglie is?"

"Yeah," said Whitey. "He lives on my block. He goes to Columbia High School. What does he have to do with this?"

"Ever notice his voice?"

"It's deep!" said Whitey. "He sings bass with the men in our church choir."

"Right," continued Gil. "Sal has agreed to call Mr. Alston and say he's from the Water Department. Then he explained what Sal was going to tell the principal.

Whitey said, "I know Sal, you guys. If anybody can do this, he can. He's a very wild and funny dude."

Kelly asked, "Well, if there are no grown-ups, how do we get into the school?"

Phil jumped in before Gil had a chance to answer. "It's easy. There is an old window at the back of the playground under the library . . . the window with three jail bars in front of it. The window is always left open just a crack—we think for air circulation. It's the kind that swings open from the side when you push in. I'm small enough to squeeze through those bars; then I can open the school doors from the inside."

"Isn't that against the law?" someone asked.

Phil answered, "Well, we're not going to steal anything, we're just going to teach students."

"How are we supposed to know what to teach?" asked Bobby.

Gil replied, "Whatever class you're assigned to teach, you have to watch and listen to beforehand. Find out what they're working on. Kids with sisters and brothers in other grades can look at their homework and ask them what they're doing at school. Plus, remember the games and stuff you learned when you were in that grade. You can make up stuff too, but just be sure you don't do anything that could get us in trouble."

Someone else asked, "What if someone gets sick? They might need a real nurse."

"Well, Leo got some kind of award for first aid in Cub Scouts. Right, Leo?"

"Yep!"

"He'll be the nurse. If someone gets really sick, we'll just have to quit and call 911 or the kid's house. That hardly ever happens, though. It should be a normal day."

Leo offered a question. "The school phone rings all day long. What do we do if someone wants to talk to a teacher or Mr. Alston?"

Gil replied, "I guess the best thing is to say they can't come to the phone right now, take the number, and tell them they'll call back."

They continued to discuss other possible problems and offered more ways to solve them. When the questions ended, Gil said, "Well, what about it? Are you willing to give it a try? If you want to drop out, okay, but you have to tell me by Monday."

They all agreed to think about it. Gil spoke with more enthusiasm than before. "Today's Friday. Let's meet here after school on Monday. If enough of us show up, we'll decide who does what. Then we'll have from Tuesday to

Thursday to get ready. Friday will be Takeover Day. That's one week from today."

"That doesn't give us much time to get ready," someone shouted.

Gil responded, "I think we've gotta do it fast before someone finds out. Everyone here has to promise not to tell anyone anything about this. If this leaks out to even one person, we'll get caught. Okay, that's it. By Monday you should decide if you want to be involved and which grade you want to teach. On Tuesday we start final preparations."

* * *

Over the weekend, each student imagined what Takeover Day would be like. They had a billion thoughts and some cool ideas.

"What if my class doesn't do what I tell them?"

"Will I use the whiteboard? Computers?"

"I get to grade papers. Cool!"

"Will I know any of my students?"

"Uh oh! What if I have a kid who cries or throws up?"

"I could be famous!"

"What's going to happen to us when everyone finds out?"

"Will I get into real serious trouble? Like suspended from school?"

Every one of them was tense and excited at the same time. They loved having such a big secret.

A New Central School Staff

Everyone was early for the secret meeting at Cameron Field on Monday afternoon. No one had dropped out of the takeover plan. They were all standing around an old picnic table when Gil started the meeting. "Wow," he said. His voice was low and shaky from excitement. "Okay then, everyone is here, so let's get started. Who wants kindergarten?"

The meeting went smoothly. There was no arguing over assignments, but not everyone was confident. Sadie took the job of fourth-grade teacher. She explained to everyone, "I really want to do this, but I'm not too sure I can. I mean, what happens if they ask me questions I can't answer or something like that?

"Sadie, you'll be fine," said Gil. "You are smart enough for them."

Priscilla was blunt. "Sadie, don't be such a wimp. All you have to do is give them some work to do and tell them to be quiet. Anybody can do it."

Sadie blushed and in a weak voice she said, "Okay, I'll do it."

Gil was surprised to see that Sarah decided to be involved. "Sarah, do you really want to teach second grade? You're usually very quiet."

Sarah spoke out with surprising energy. "Yes, I want to do it! I have already started thinking about what I'll teach."

Gil was pleasantly surprised. "Okay then, great! Good luck!"

* * *

The next day, Tuesday, some of the fifth-grade students were quieter than usual. Bobby didn't crack his usual jokes. Students whispered to each other. More students asked Mrs. Garcia for washroom requests, and those washroom trips took a little longer than usual. No one noticed that they walked more slowly in the hallways, and sometimes they peeked into classrooms and listened.

Mr. Winter, the school custodian, spotted a kid hanging around his office. "Need help, young man? Are you a spy or something?" he joked. The boy shook his head and hurried away.

"Hey, what's your name?" asked the custodian.

"Whitey!" he answered. "Uh, I gotta go," he said over his shoulder as he hustled back to his room.

Mrs. Parry, the school secretary, also noted a couple of students entering and leaving the office more often than usual. When one showed up for the third time, she asked,

"What is it you need, young man?" The boy rushed out the door. Mrs. Parry heard a snapping sound.

It was one thirty. Mrs. Garcia sat back and looked over her fifth-grade class while they were writing sentences using spelling words. Priscilla was adjusting her hair, as usual. Sadie was getting some help with a spelling word from Dusty. Sarah was sitting alone, quietly working. Leo and Bobby were writing. Their teacher thought, "It's so peaceful in here. They're working so well. What is going on?"

"May I get something from my locker?" asked Phil.

"Yes, Phil, go ahead."

Mrs. Garcia didn't quite know what was happening or why. She thought, "That's it! More kids are asking to leave the room." She then shook her head slightly. "Oh stop it, Cindy. Enjoy it while it lasts."

Meanwhile, during Phil's walk down the hallway, he found the basement door slightly open. He reached in and grabbed the doorknob on the basement side. It turned easily. He discovered that the door wasn't locked on either side.

Carl also noticed that something in the classroom seemed different. He whispered to his pal Wes Westrum, "There's a lot of whispering going on in here. Something's up, and I bet Hodges has something to do with it."

Wes looked around the room. "What! I don't see anything."

Carl answered, "That's because you never notice what's going on. I'm the one that tells you what's happening, and I know you and me and Duke haven't been invited. It definitely smells like another Hodges scheme of some kind."

Near the end of the day, Mrs. Garcia noticed that it was still quieter than usual. She thought, "This weirdness has been going on all day. I want to just enjoy it, but there has got to be more to this than I'm seeing. Maybe."

Final Plans

The next day, Wednesday, Mrs. Garcia found that the students were behaving normally again. "Aha! We're back to our usual selves today; and not as many bathroom requests either. Hmm!" She thought that whatever caused Tuesday's weirdness had stopped. There was still some whispering going on, but Mrs. Garcia didn't mind. "It was a little strange yesterday, but it's over now. All these minor issues that ten-year-olds have come and go. Kids are kids. I've been teaching long enough to know not to get too excited about this kind of behavior. And look at them. They are working so nicely."

She decided that she would ease up on their workload at the end of the week. "I'll make Friday an easier day for them; maybe even give them a longer recess. It would be a nice reward for such good behavior."

* * *

On the following day, Thursday, the "teachers" met at Cameron Field after school. "I'm all set," said Bobby. "I got work for my third graders that will take all day. Third grade seems so easy."

"Phil says he'll have no trouble getting his skinny body through those bars," chuckled Gil. He smiled and continued, "He's practicing his bending and stretching on the jungle gym. Says he knows how to unlock the school doors with something called an Allen wrench that's in the secretary's desk."

Gil added, "Telephones will be covered. Everyone should be here by eight fifteen. I just hope all of our parents believe our stories about why we're coming to school early."

Dusty said, "Gil, I don't think we can do any more to get ready. We just have to let it happen. This is weird. I feel scared and excited at the same time."

After the meeting broke up, Gil and Dusty began their walk home. "I sure hope everybody does their job," Gil said it like he was praying. "One screw-up and the whole day will fall apart—and that means big trouble for all of us."

Dusty was more hopeful. "Naw, it's going to be good. Just wait. Has anyone backed out?"

"Nope! We're all in. We even have some extra people, so I gave them jobs in the cafeteria. They will fill in if anyone chickens out at the last minute."

"Good!"

Dusty said, "I've been listening all week to the way Mrs. Parry talks on the phone, and I've practiced how I'll answer the phone, but it still makes me nervous."

"Yeah, I know. I'm nervous too. The worst would be that Stoney or some teacher comes to school anyway. That would kill the whole thing."

"Boy!" Dusty almost whispered, "I never thought of that."

Gil's confidence returned. "When we do this, Stoney will get the shock of his life. You're right, Dusty. The only thing left now is to just do it."

The person they were talking about, Mr. Alston, just happened to be looking out his office window as Gil and Dusty passed by. He said to himself, "Now there go a couple of nice boys!"

* * *

Students' Roles

Gil Hodges	PRINCIPAL
Dusty Rhodes	SECRETARY
Leo Durocher	NURSE
Phil Rizzuto	GYM TEACHER
Whitey Lockman	CUSTODIAN
Priscilla Wright	KINDERGARTEN TEACHER
Dylan Hunt	FIRST-GRADE TEACHER
Sarah Glum	SECOND-GRADE TEACHER
Bobby Thompson	THIRD-GRADE TEACHER
Sadie Harding	FOURTH-GRADE TEACHER
Kelly Driten	FIFTH-GRADE TEACHER

Phone Calls and Visitors

Gil and Dusty stood in the office and watched the flow of children pass by the office door. None of them seemed to notice that there was not one adult in sight. It was 8:52 A.M., and the takeover was starting smoothly. It took only a few minutes for the crowd to dwindle to a few stragglers. After they had all passed by, Gil stepped out into the front hallway. Then he poked his head back into the office. "Hey, Dusty, I'm going to check out the hallways . . . see how things are going."

"Okay!"

"Leo's in the nurse's office if you need help with anything."

"Okay," Dusty repeated.

Gil walked very slowly down the fifth-grade hallway, but stayed away from his own room. He knew his classmates would ask him why he wasn't joining them. Locker doors were opening and closing, and some students were chatting. Everyone was disappearing into classrooms.

"Good! No questions yet. No problems so far. This side of the school is good." He went on to check the rest of the school.

* * *

Dusty was pacing back and forth near his office desk. "Why isn't the phone ringing?" He pulled his chair closer to the desk and looked at the three buttons on the phone. They should be flashing soon. He imagined that he would probably be taking messages all day long. "These phones ring constantly. Oh brother! What are Mom and Dad and Grandpa going to say when they find out what I've been doing? I've never done anything like this before. They'll probably ground me for a month. Oh geez!"

Snap!

His mom and dad were strict, but they never yelled when he got in trouble. He began thinking about the cool things his parents and he did together, like taking driving trips and camping. They took him to old caves and science museums. He loved the computer games they gave him. His dad taught him how to play chess and bought him miniature rockets, which they launched at Gillson Park. He loved the whooshing sound of the rockets when they shot into the sky. The rockets went a thousand feet straight up, then floated down under tiny parachutes. Dusty smiled when he remembered his dad climbing a tree to rescue one of his rockets. They did a lot together. Now, here he is sneaking into his school and helping to take it over. He couldn't let his pal, Gil, do all this without him.

* * *

In the next office Leo found out where the bandages were kept. He knew the little kids loved getting Band-Aids. He also went through the desk drawers to find scissors, tape, alcohol, and other stuff that the nurse uses. When he thought that he was ready, he just sat down at his desk and waited.

Sure enough, students began trickling in with their attendance books. He said, "Thank you," to each of them and took the books. The little kids, who were very shy, turned and quickly went back to their rooms. Leo opened each book, pretending he was doing the nurse's job. The nurse always checked to see who was absent.

Next door, the office phone rang with its loud, electronic tone. Dusty was so nervous he jumped out of his chair and then sat back down again, as rigid as a manikin in a department store. He had one thumb curled under a suspender and the other hand on the receiver. On the third ring, he yanked the receiver off its cradle and pressed it to his ear.

"Good morning! Central School. May I help you?" He hoped he didn't sound rattled.

"Good morning. This is Mrs. Keren. May I speak to Mr. Alston, please?" Mrs. Keren was the principal of Harper School, which was about two miles away.

"Uh, he's not in right now, uh, today. May I take a message?"

"Is Mr. Alston sick?" she asked. "He looked fine yesterday."

"Oh no! He's not sick. He's away for a special meeting. He'll be back on Monday for sure."

"Where is Mrs. Parry? Is she sick?"

"Uh, Mrs. Parry isn't in the office now. I'm answering the phone for her. She's very busy since the principal is not here. May I take a message?" Dusty wanted to end this conversation as quickly as possible.

"Well," Mrs. Keren said, "just tell him I called. It's nothing urgent. Thank you."

"Yes, Ma'am! Good-bye." He put the phone down, sat back in the chair, and slapped his leg. "Hey, this isn't so tough after all!" Right away he grabbed notepaper and jotted down the message, "Mrs. Keren called. Nothing urgent."

The second call was from the Contented Cow Dairy Company. A nice lady said, "This is Sally over at Contented Cow. The milk delivery truck will be there on Wednesday. Please tell the cafeteria ladies."

"Okay," he answered. Dusty wrote a second note to the custodian. "I'll drop it off in his office at lunch." His confidence was skyrocketing.

At 9:25 A.M. a book salesman called and asked to speak with the principal. Dusty took his number and said he'd call back next week. In the first hour he had answered the phone fourteen times and written a message for each call. "Now I understand why my dad says he takes vacations to get away from telephones."

* * *

Earlier, Gil had returned from his inspection tour and asked Dusty, "Everything okay here?"

"Fine so far. I'm getting a lot of calls. No problems. I think I would be a very good secretary," he joked. "How's it look in the classrooms?"

"It's awesome, Dusty! It's early, but it looks like nobody is freaking out about not having grown-ups in the school. I'm still nervous, though." Gil held up his hand, waving two crossed fingers. "Here's hoping! I think I'll check out Mr. Alston's office again."

He walked into the principal's small office and sat right down at the huge desk. As his eyes scanned the room, he noticed a framed family picture on the wall. Mr. Alston and his wife were smiling, posed with their son and daughter in their best clothes. "Mr. Alston is a father? I never thought about that!"

Gil slowly turned his head to inspect everything in the office. There were bookshelves filled with hundreds of books and education magazines. There were plants and more pictures of his children taken at different ages. There was students' framed artwork hanging on the walls. Names and dates were printed at the bottom of each. "I never thought he cared about artwork. He's always so busy yelling at us. Hmm. I wouldn't mind having one of my drawings up there."

Then he stopped that kind of thinking and focused on what he was doing. He tilted his head onto the back of the leather chair, crossed his legs, and rocked a little, enjoying the moment.

In an instant his thoughts reversed and he sat straight up in the chair. He remembered that days before he had held dark thoughts of how today could all fall apart, that he would miss some important detail in the planning. He thought about students refusing to work. He pictured first graders who were scared and crying. He imagined students running and shouting in the hallways and maybe even fighting. Then he relaxed a little. He told himself, "Take it easy. It's almost nine thirty, and so far so good."

He put his head back and began rocking again. Somehow his fifth-grade "teachers" had convinced the students to go along with the takeover. He made himself relax in the chair as his thoughts turned to what a principal's job should be. "All you have to do is be strict with the kids, hire teachers, and buy things for the school. That's not so hard."

He sat a while longer, gazing out the school window. He saw the mailman talking to Mrs. Preston in front of her house across the street. They waved good-bye to each other, and the mailman turned to leave.

Suddenly Gil shot out of the chair like he had been pushed. He stared out the window with huge eyes. The mailman was walking toward the school. "Oh no! He's coming in here!" He kicked over a wastepaper basket as he ran into the office. "Dusty," he shouted. "We're in trouble! The mailman's on his way here! He's coming to the front door."

Dusty froze like he was staring at a tyrannosaurus rex. They turned their heads to watch the monitor, waiting for the mailman to appear on the screen. Gil had no idea that this would be the first of four unwelcome visitors in the school that day.

* * *

The mailman's face appeared on the monitor. When he rang the doorbell, Dusty pushed the button to buzz him in. The boys were frozen stiff with terror. When the mailman walked slowly into the office, his eyes scanned the room. He was looking for Mrs. Parry. Instead he saw two nervous ten-year-olds staring at him like they were looking at a ghost. He placed a stack of mail on Dusty's desk. "Morning boys!" he said pleasantly.

"Good morning!" Gil answered in a voice that sounded like a recorded phone message.

"Where is my friend Mrs. Parry?"

Gil's heart pounded. He spoke as calmly as he could. "She asked a couple of us to watch the office while she was gone. She had to take some papers to a teacher. Do you need to talk to her?"

"Oh no, I'm just used to giving her the mail."

Dusty hooked his suspenders and stared off into space. Gil explained, "She said she would be gone about ten minutes," He pretended to brag, "She put us in charge."

The mailman's eyes shifted between the two boys, then scanned the room. "Well, you guys are doing a fine job. Okay, guess I'd better get going. Tell her I said hi when she comes back."

"I sure will. Bye!" replied Gil.

As the mailman stepped into the hallway, the school doorbell rang again. They saw on the monitor that it was Mrs. Preston from across the street. The mailman opened the door for her, and the boys could hear their conversation from the office.

"Oh, Danny," she said, "I forgot to tell you. John and I will be at the board meeting on Tuesday night. Would you and Laura like to go out with us for pie and coffee afterward? We can talk about the fund-raiser." She never took her eyes off the mailman.

"Sure, Mary. I'll ask Laura."

"Good!" she exclaimed. They said good-bye to each other, and Mrs. Preston entered the office.

"Oh hello, boys."

"Hello, Mrs. Preston."

"Hey, where's Mrs. Parry?"

"She's with a teacher now. We're watching the office while she's gone."

Mrs. Preston looked around the office. "Well, looks like you're doing a good job. Be sure to tell her I stopped by. Okay?"

Gil nodded his head quickly and said, "Yes, Ma'am, we'll tell her." She was gone in a moment.

"Phew!" gasped Dusty. They gazed at her through the window until she crossed the street. "That was close! I'm glad you were here, Gil. I would have wet my pants if I was alone. You acted so cool! Think they suspected any-thing?"

"I sure hope not. It would be really bad if they did, especially after such a good start."

The phone rang again, and again they looked at each other as if they were saying, "Uh oh, here's another prob-lem." On the second ring, Dusty reached for the phone, forced a smile and said, "Good morning, Central School. May I help you?" Gil listened. Dusty said, "We start at nine o'clock, Ma'am, and end at three." Dusty gave Gil the thumbs-up sign, and Gil retreated back into the princi-pal's office. All was well, so far.

Students React

Kelly was in charge of Mrs. Garcia's fifth-grade class. When her classmates first entered the room, her knees were shaking. She didn't sit in the teacher's chair. She was sure they would all want to know why she was sitting there and ask where Mrs. Garcia was. She stood near the front of the room, taking a few steps here and there, wringing her sweaty hands. "I'll never get through this!" flashed through her mind.

She said hi to a couple of friends who greeted her, but they didn't question why she wasn't in her seat. Then someone asked, "Hey, why all the empty seats?" Everyone looked around the room.

Somebody else added, "Yeah, a bunch of kids are absent today!"

One of them noticed Kelly pacing. "Hey, Kelly! Where is Mrs. Garcia? What's going on, Kel? Why are you up there?"

One of them said, "I know. Mrs. Garcia got caught in traffic. Again."

Kelly's became very serious. She raised both hands, palms facing the students. "Mrs. Garcia isn't going to be here today."

Someone shouted, "Is she sick?"

Another asked, "Where's the sub?"

Kelly responded, "There is no sub. I am going to be the teacher today."

"Ha ha! Oh sure. Like you're smart enough to teach us!"

They saw that she wasn't joking by the look on her face. "Are you serious?" asked one of the girls.

"Yes, I'm serious. I'm going to take over for Mrs. Garcia. She isn't here. After we do the Pledge we'll start with Math groups just like she does, then do Reading, and so on."

Wes asked, "You mean all day?"

"Yes!" she almost shouted.

"Why? What's happening?" asked someone else.

She explained. "Students are taking over the school today. There aren't any grown-ups in the building."

All movement stopped. Eyes were wide, and mouths dropped open. "You're kidding us! She's stuck in traffic again," said a boy sitting up front.

"No," Kelly shook her head. "It's just us. We want to show Stoney and Mrs. Dower that we're old enough to do important jobs by ourselves. Remember how they treat us like babies? Taking our good games away? We're doing this to show them we deserve more credit."

The same student said, "So, zero teachers are in the school right now?"

Kelly nodded her head.

"All day?"

Kelly nodded again.

"Great! Party time! Let's have recess all day!" he shouted. "This is cool."

All of the students began talking at once. "Games all day! It's a miracle! This is awesome!" A few began getting up from their seats.

Kelly put her hands on her hips and shouted, "Wait! Just listen for a minute!" The noise stopped immediately. "We can have recess and some fun stuff, but we gotta keep this a regular school day. We gotta do the work."

"Oh no! Boo! Why do we have to work if there's no teacher?"

Kelly told them the whole story. She tried hard to convince them how important it was for them to do school work to prove their point. The kids who were standing slowly sat down again.

"Well, we can have *some* fun, can't we?" asked one of the boys.

"Sure, as long as we get our work done and have something to show Mrs. Garcia when she returns on Monday." As they listened, Kelly's voice got stronger. "Come on! If we do this it will change everything! We will earn their respect. They'll stop pushing us around."

Daryl asked, "Are we still going to have Science today?"

Kelly knew that Daryl had some kind of experiment for today's science class. "Yes, Daryl. We'll have Science this afternoon."

Someone else said, "I don't like this. I want some grown-ups here in case something bad happens."

"Like what?" asked another.

"Like if someone faints, or there's a fire."

"Oh, that's not going to happen. When's the last time there was a fire in this school? Probably never."

Kelly said, "We have made plans for emergencies, but we are hoping that it's just a normal day and nothing weird happens."

"Wow, not a teacher anywhere. No one's ever done that before!"

"Yeah! A teacher-free day."

Almost everyone was smiling, but Carl had a different reaction. "Oh! So that's why some of you were acting so mysterious this week!" He told the rest of the class how he'd noticed whispering and the long walks in the hallway.

"Hey," Duke Snyder complained. "Why weren't we included?"

Kelly looked nervous again. "Well, I don't know. I guess there weren't enough jobs for everyone. Ask Gil and Dusty. It was their idea."

Everyone began talking at once, asking who the other "teachers" were for this day. The noise in the room was as loud as the cafeteria at lunchtime. Kelly overheard one student say, "I think we should have at least one real teacher here in case there's trouble."

Another answered, "Are you crazy? This can be the best day of the year. No teachers!"

Carl, Wes, and Duke were complaining to each other. "I don't like being left out. Who decided who the teachers would be, anyway?" A piece of paper flew across the room. Some were yelling. Suddenly Kelly cupped her hands around her mouth and screamed, "Wait, everybody! Quiet!"

The room became silent again. "We are all going to lose out if we don't do this right." She growled. "At least try. This could be the best school day ever if we don't mess it up. Doing work is what we have to do. It will show them that we are mature."

The kids were quiet, like they were thinking it over. Kelly said calmly, "Let's start . . . now . . . and I'll tell Gil about what you said." She looked at one of the girls. "Jennifer, it's your turn. Would you . . . like . . . lead us in the Pledge?"

Without thinking about it, Jennifer stood up, faced the flag, and sure enough everyone followed the routine, hands over hearts. "I pledge allegiance to the flag of the . . . ." Kelly closed her eyes and sighed. She listened as they recited the Pledge. She thought about how things were going better than she had imagined. She had pictured students running in the rooms and hallways, roughhousing in the gym and lunchroom, even walking out and going home. She hoped it would stay this way.

" . . . with liberty and justice for all."

Everyone sat right down, just like they did every day, but their eyes were glued on Kelly. She grabbed a stack of math papers she had prepared and handed them out to pupils near the front of the room. She declared in a firm voice, "We can do this, everybody! This is going to work.

The other classes are working too." "I hope!" she thought to herself.

The students wrote their names and the date, just like Mrs. Garcia insisted. They all began doing multiplication and division problems. Carl didn't start on the math work when he got his paper. He watched the others as they were busy writing. No one noticed his angry look.

The Teacher Winked Like It Was a Secret

Priscilla had her kindergarten room ready well before the bell rang. There were toys set up in the different areas of the room, crayons and markers were ready, paste and paper were at hand, and music was playing. She looked outside the entry door and saw the mothers and their children waiting to enter the school.

Suddenly she shot both hands to her mouth like she was trying to stop from squealing. "Oh no!" she whispered aloud. "Some of those mothers are going to walk their children all the way into the classrooms. They'll be looking for Miss Melody."

Her hands dropped to her sides. "Aha! That's it!" She opened a box of cookies she had planned to serve later in the morning, put them on two paper plates, and set them down on the play tables.

When the 8:50 A.M. bell sounded, the kindergarten entrance became a beehive of activity, with lively children spilling into the hallway. Parents kissed their kids good-bye, then stood to watch their little ones walk through the entrance. Two of the mothers approached the door, ready to take their kids to the room. Both five-year-olds were holding their mothers' hands. Priscilla allowed the children who were walking to the room on their own to pass by her. She said, "Hi, everybody. Hang your jacket on a hook and help yourself to one cookie. I'll be right in with you." She met the two moms at the doorway, looking as confident and cheery as she could.

"Good morning." She looked right at the mothers, then at their children. Priscilla leaned forward to talk to the two little girls. "Miss Melody asked me to come out here and speak to you and your moms." She looked up to the moms, then quickly back to the girls. "Today is a very special day in kindergarten. All of the children are walking into class on their own to show how grown up they are." Priscilla held out her hands to the children, hoping they would join her. The girls held their mothers' hands more tightly. They looked worried.

The mothers smiled at each other, then looked back at the fifth grader. Priscilla squatted down very close to the girls' faces. In a low voice she said, "The teacher has a special treat for you to eat in the classroom," and winked at them like it was a secret. The girls looked interested, but kept their grips. Even more quietly, she said, "It's cookies. You can have one right now if you go in together without your moms," she whispered.

The kids looked at each other. One released her mother's hand and began walking. She turned around and waved. "Bye, Mommy." She looked at her friend. "C'mon, Anna." The other girl smiled at her mom and then joined her friend. When Priscilla stood up, one of the mothers said, "Nicely done, young lady." They turned and left. She heard one of the moms saying, "Well, that was easy."

Priscilla followed the two girls into the room. She saw that the kids were eating cookies around the table, talking and giggling. "Itsy Bitsy Spider" was playing on the CD player. She was relieved that the parents didn't ask about Miss Melody. Both girls happily joined their classmates, grabbed their cookies, and became totally involved in their conversations. Priscilla said to everyone, "When you are finished with your cookie, come and join me on the rug."

* * *

Bobby was in charge of Mr. Wilkins's third-grade classroom. He had never been in charge of anything in his life, except maybe being the goofiest kid in the class. He found that preparing lessons for this class wasn't as difficult as he had imagined. The toughest part had been finding out what they were studying. Now he was watching "his" students come into their classroom. He knew many of Mr. Wilkins's students from the playground and the neighborhood. "Hmm. They look bigger when they're in the classroom and littler when they're on the playground."

When the nine o'clock bell rang, none of the students were sitting at their desks. He was counting on it being quiet with everyone in his or her seat, just like in Mrs. Garcia's room. She was strict about that. These students were spread out all over the room, talking and laughing.

He walked over to the light switch near the doorway and flicked the lights on and off twice. Immediately the noise level dropped. Everyone looked at him. In a voice higher than usual he announced, "Sit down, everyone. I have a special announcement to make!"

"Hi, Bobby," came a greeting from a boy who lived four houses from him.

He answered, "Hi, Chuck," in a quieter voice.

Three other students said hello. He stood at the head of the class and put two fingers up, like they do at Cub Scout meetings.

Everyone became quiet. Bobby came right to the point. "I am going to be your teacher today. Mr. Wilkins is absent." He said it firmly and confidently, with a smile.

They didn't move. Some looked confused. "Wait!" said one boy. "Are you kidding?"

Bobby told them the whole story about showing parents that the students can do work on their own. "This is our chance to show everyone we won't fall apart when we need to get work done." They stared at him quietly and listened to what he had to say. "This won't work unless you do the normal school work I give you today. Are you willing to do that?"

"Okay," said Monte, the smartest kid in the class. "I'll do it. This is too cool!"

"Wow, no grown-ups bossing us! C'mon, everybody, let's do it!" said someone else.

Those two comments set the mood for the class to accept the idea. Alvin Dark, the class athlete, followed with, "This will be awesome!" He grabbed a pencil from his desk and asked, "What do we do first, Bobby?"

Bobby said, "Math book, page fifty-four."

Rigid to Relaxed

Sarah was at the teacher's desk when the 8:50 A.M. bell rang. She watched her second graders walk by as they entered the room. Some gave her quick glances; others talked to friends and didn't notice her. No one seemed interested in Sarah being there.

She recognized some of the children from her neighborhood. She wanted to say hi, but something kept her from talking. At the sound of the bell at nine o'clock, she stepped forward and announced sternly to those still standing, "Sit down now so we can get started!"

The seven-year-olds began to look puzzled, but settled into their seats. "Where is Mrs. Geiger?" asked one of the girls.

"She won't be here today. I am filling in for her. Fifth graders are teaching all the classes today."

"Not really," the girl giggled.

"Yes, really. It's a special day," said Sarah. She sounded serious. "You must stay in your seats and work quietly on today's lessons. You must complete all the work. If everyone is good, maybe we can have game time later. Won't that be fun?"

The second graders said nothing, trying to figure out what this was all about. Others looked around, hoping to find their teacher hiding in the back of the room. "Is this a joke?" asked one of the boys.

"No, this is serious." Sarah explained how it all got started and how important it was that everyone cooperate. One little boy began crying, saying, "I want Mrs. Geiger."

A girl asked, "But what if something bad happens? There should be a real teacher here to take care of us."

"We've made plans for that," replied Sarah. She ignored the crying boy. "Don't worry. Nothing bad will happen. All you have to do is get your work done. I will help you.

Sarah led the class in the Pledge of Allegiance. When they sat down she said, "It's time to get started. We'll do Reading first, like you always do. I have an assignment for you." Sarah handed out the papers she had prepared and asked them to read the short paragraphs and answer the questions. The students took the papers and began reading. The kid who was crying quieted down to sniffling and started on the paper.

It was all going smoothly for a few minutes. Everyone read quietly and began to write answers to the questions. Sarah sat at her desk and watched. Soon some of the boys began whispering and giggling.

"Roger Maris and Tony Kubek, get back to work right now. No talking!"

They quieted down but not for long. Moments later some of the girls began to whisper. Eventually, it seemed like half of the kids were not doing their assignments. Some of the boys got up to visit friends at their desks.

"Christopher, Eric, and Mark, get back to your seats and finish your reading. Tammy and Merrilee, you've been talking to each other and you haven't finished your worksheets." She scolded a few other pupils. The more she scolded, the more the whispering and giggling increased. One of the boys spoke up. "We don't really have to do what you say. You're just a student in this school."

A few others agreed. "Yeah!"

Sarah looked confused. It was all falling apart. She wanted to scream at them to get back to work, but she knew that would make things worse. Without warning, her eyes filled with tears and she began to cry softly. She tried to stop, but the tears came anyway. Her chest was jerking up and down with each breath. She held her hands over her face.

The students' eyes were on her, waiting, like they didn't know what to do. After a minute, one of the girls slid from her chair and walked up to Sarah at the front of the room. She offered Sarah a tissue. Sarah took it and blew her nose hard, saying, "I can't do this."

The girl stated, "They're being mean to you because you are being mean to us."

Sarah cried, "What?"

The girl just looked at her, smiled, and nodded her head up and down. Sarah answered, "But I don't know what else to do! Everyone keeps talking."

The class listened quietly. The little girl continued, "Be nice to us. We like having you in charge, but not if you are going to be mean."

Sarah dried her eyes, and blew her nose again. She looked up at the children staring at her. "I'm sorry!" she blurted out. "I'm not sure how to do this." She looked at the little girl who was standing next to her. After a pause, Sarah just shrugged her shoulders and smiled. She said, "Okay, I get it. Thank you!" It was barely a whisper. The second grader returned the smile and walked back to her seat. Sarah stood straight up, looked directly at her students, took a big breath with her hands at her sides, and assured them with confidence, "I'll be better."

There was a new, relaxed feeling from the students, and some whispers. Sarah spotted more smiles, and that made her feel even better. Using a kind teacher-voice she asked, "Would you please do your work now? It would be great if we could make our special students' day be successful. I'll try to help you if I can, and I will try very hard not to be mean." The girl that gave Sarah the tissue picked up her paper and began reading. The rest of the students did the same.

Sarah watched them work for a short time, then sighed and returned to the teacher's desk. Minutes later some boys began talking to each other and giggling. Sarah peeked at them and then looked away. She was very relieved when they soon went back to work on their own.

* * *

Sometime later Dusty left the office for his own inspection tour. "I want to see what's happening in this school for myself," he told Gil. He peeked into every room he passed. When he came to Sarah's classroom, he walked in to say a quick hello. Sarah was correcting papers while the students worked. A few were talking quietly with others. He tiptoed up to her desk.

"Hi! How are you doing?" he whispered.

"Good," she said in a low voice. "I had a bad start, but I think it's going to be okay now. How's it going in the office?"

"A whole lot of phone calls, but I'm good." Dusty looked at the class as he walked out. He liked the way Sarah was running things. Sarah heard the gentle snap in the hallway after he left their room.

Leo Really Knows What He Is Doing

From the minute Phil learned that he got the gym teacher's job, he knew how he would teach his classes. He understood that kids like to run around in the gym, but with no adults around they might go crazy. Mr. Mays had a rule. When he blew his whistle during class, you had to freeze where you stood. No exceptions. If you didn't freeze you had to do a lot of push-ups. Phil decided to follow that rule and hoped it would work. He thought that playing kickball in the gym was the safest activity to do. It was also the most popular game at school.

Phil's 9:45 A.M. gym period was Mr. Wilkins's third-grade class. Bobby brought them to the gym, and they ran in like wild horses, hooting, cheering, and sliding on the floor. A few of the boys yelled, "Hi, Phil! Wow! You're our gym teacher." They began cheering. Phil blew hard on the whistle, and they froze to instant silence.

"Okay!" he hollered. "Begin four laps around the gym, no racing, no passing!" He used the same tone as Mr. Mays. The entire class jogged the four laps while they talked and laughed. When they stopped, Phil led them in the regular stretching exercises. When he announced kickball for the period, everyone cheered. "Teams one and three bat first, and teams two and four are in the field." Some kids complained that those teams were unfair, but Phil was ready for them. "Tell it to Mr. Mays on Monday."

"Mr. Mays won't care," was the response.

Phil shrugged his shoulders and said, "That's your problem. Right now, take the field." It wasn't long before everyone was in place and the pitcher was ready to roll the first pitch.

Phil enjoyed being the umpire, and he was good at it. He stood on the sideline between third base and home. His whistle was on a string around his neck. He was small, but he was tough. He yelled to the pitcher, "Okay, roll it over home plate!"

The batter yelled to the pitcher, "Slow and bouncy!"

The pitcher delivered the maroon ball like he was bowling. The first batter kicked the ball so hard it made a splatting sound when it smacked into the far wall of the gym. Phil watched every play, calling runners safe and out. Phil kept track of time so this class would be ready to return to their room when the next group arrived. They had thirty minutes to play the game.

Alvin was yelling every time someone on his team kicked the ball. He was a kid who played every game like his life depended on it. "Run! Run!" he'd scream as loud as he could. His neck veins bulged out when he shouted. His buddies nicknamed him "Lungs."

The game was loud and fast-moving. With three minutes left in the period, and his team losing by three runs,

Alvin came up to bat. There were two outs, and bases were loaded. He set up behind home plate with a determined look in his eyes. His teammates were screaming, "Alvin! Alvin! Alvin!"

On the first pitch he flattened the ball with his right foot. It sailed the length of the gym on a fly and flattened against the wall. His teammates were screaming and jumping as runners scored. The ball was finally controlled and thrown in as Alvin rounded third. The ball came flying in toward Alvin as he slid hard. He was off-balance and hit the floor awkwardly, then rolled over a few times at home plate. He was safe. They all gathered around, and some of them piled on top of him, fluffing his hair and pulling at his clothes.

When they tried to help him up, they saw that Alvin was in trouble. He was holding his right arm straight along his side. His face showed pain. *"Owww!"* he yelled, and laid back down. "My arm."

Phil quickly ran over as the students gathered around. "Everybody back! barked Phil. "Let him breathe!" His teammates took a step backward in a circle around Alvin. Phil knelt down next to him.

"Owww! It hurts! *Owww!"* He kept his arm straight.

"Can you bend it?" Phil asked. Alvin tried very slowly to bend the arm. He was able to move it a little but let out a painful cry. Phil was afraid the arm might be broken. He helped Alvin up and yelled, "Everyone line up at the door."

The students walked quickly to the door, but kept their eyes on Alvin. They quieted down as they watched. Phil stayed with Alvin, who had begun to cry.

Bobby returned to pick up his class, and everyone shouted to him, "Alvin's hurt! He broke his arm!"

"What!" Bobby said. When he looked at Alvin, Phil said, "Take your class back to your room. I'll take Alvin to the nurse's office."

"Okay!" Bobby replied, and motioned them to follow him.

When his class was gone, Alvin tried to bend his arm again. "*Ahh!* It hurts." He hung onto Phil's shoulder with his good arm as they began their walk to the office. Alvin murmured, "I think it's broken! It's broken! I won't be able to play peewee basketball." He began crying a little harder.

In the nurse's office, Leo was looking at the pictures on the snakebite page in an old first-aid book. When Phil and Alvin appeared at the door, Leo jumped straight up. "What happened?"

As Phil spoke, he guided his patient to the couch. "Alvin hurt his arm. He was sliding but then rolled over himself a couple of times." Alvin sat down moaning and holding the bad arm. Phil said, "Hey, Leo, I gotta get back to the gym. Can you take care of him?"

"Yeah, go ahead, Phil."

Leo remembered his first-aid training. He said, "Alvin, lie down on the couch and put your feet up on this pillow." He covered him with a blanket. Alvin held his arm straight against his side. He stared at Leo. "It hurts!"

Leo asked, "Where?"

Alvin pointed to his elbow.

Leo looked at the arm and touched it in various places. It looked normal: no unusual bends, no swelling. "Try to bend your arm at the elbow as much as you can."

Alvin looked worried, but his arm moved normally and with less pain. "Good!" said Leo. "Stay there and relax. I'll make an ice pack for you to hold onto for a while. Keep the swelling down. I don't think it's broken. How do you feel?"

"Better," answered Alvin. He was calm now and not as scared. Leo said, "Put this ice right on the elbow."

"Okay."

Leo said, "I'll be right back."

He took a few steps into the office where Dusty and Gil were talking. "I've got Alvin from Mr. Wilkins's class on the bed. He hurt his arm in gym, but I think he's okay." Dusty and Gil hurried into the nurse's office to see the patient.

Alvin spoke softly, "I'm feeling a lot better now." All three guys stared down at him.

"Good!" said Gil.

Fifteen minutes later, Leo walked Alvin back to class. Alvin kept his sore arm hanging straight down at his side. He held the ice pack against his elbow. Leo told him, "If it swells up or starts to hurt real bad, come back to the office."

"Thanks a lot, Leo!"

When Alvin walked into his room, the class clapped and cheered. Leo smiled and announced, "It's not broken!" More cheers. He continued. "That guy, Leo, really knows what he's doing. I think he would be a good doctor."

Bobby said, "I thought maybe we would have to call an ambulance. That was a close one."

Alvin, feeling relieved, smiled as he looked around at his classmates. He bragged, "Oh, by the way, we won the game."

Carl Isn't Happy

It didn't take long for Kelly's fifth-grade class to get used to the takeover idea. The complaints and worries stopped after about ten minutes. As reading assignments were being finished, she said to the class, "Well, we've done Math, Gym, and Reading already. All we have left this morning is Language Arts. Then we go to lunch, but first, let's take a little break." She glanced at the clock. "We'll begin Language Arts at 11:05!"

The students immediately began talking with friends. Some met in small groups at different parts of the room. Others paired up. A few stayed at their desks and talked to their neighbors. Kelly sat at her desk and checked over the page numbers in the language arts book they were about to use.

Carl chose to meet with Wes and Duke in the back of the room. Carl spoke in low tones. "Man, those jerks—Gil and Dusty! They planned this whole takeover thing and never told us anything. Mr. Big Man Hodges does it again."

"Jerks," agreed Duke.

"Yeah! Dusty and his weird suspenders-snap whenever Gil speaks," added Duke. "I'm sick of them both!"

"Well, guess what!" snapped Carl. "This whole idea of theirs could backfire on them. I've been thinking." His face showed his anger. "There is a way to mess this thing up for them and maybe make us look good in the process."

"Yeah, how?" Wes and Duke asked together.

Carl took a quick look at Kelly, who was watching two students playing tic-tac-toe on the whiteboard. He turned back to his friends. "What do you think would happen if the fire alarm went off?"

"Whoa!" muttered Duke. He looked worried.

Wes answered, "Everyone would probably go outside, I guess."

Carl continued, "That's what I'm hoping for. Then we would look real good in the process."

Duke looked puzzled. "Really? How?"

"We kind of take charge. Lead people to safety and things like that. We'd be heroes."

"Yeah, but the fire department would come. We could get in big trouble," Duke warned.

"Not us, Dummy! Them!" explained Carl.

"How?"

"No one would know who pulled the alarm. It would be Gil and Dusty and their helpers who get busted."

"Yeah!" They all smiled at each other.

Kelly announced to the class, "It's 11:05! Let's get started." There were groans, but everyone slowly returned to their seats.

Carl muttered to his pals, "We'll talk at lunch."

Fourth-grade Meltdown

Sadie discovered that her fears about teaching fourth graders were unnecessary. Her students were excited about the takeover and cooperated immediately. It was almost too easy. Her well-planned math and spelling lessons went very well. The language arts exercise presented her with a new problem, however, when she wrote two sentences on the whiteboard. She said to the class, "You've been studying commas and periods this week. Let's continue with that." She pointed to the whiteboard and said, "I left out the punctuation marks in these two sentences. She held out a marker and asked a student. "Melissa, would you please take this marker and fill in the missing punctuation in the first sentence?"

"Sure!" Melissa said. Her ponytail swung side to side as she stepped up to the whiteboard. She placed a comma and a period in the sentence and even dotted an *i* before handing the marker back to Sadie.

"Thank you, Melissa. Very good!"

A few of the boys and girls rolled their eyes. They thought Sadie was playing the teacher role a little too dramatically. "And now," Sadie said, "let's fix the second sentence." She scanned the room. Hands were raised, and some of them were waving to get attention. Donny Mueller was looking down at his desk. His fingers were clasped together on the desktop. Sadie didn't know Donny very well, but she noticed that he had been quiet all morning, hardly moving in his seat. She called on him. "Donny, please come on up here and fill in the missing commas and periods in this sentence," She wanted to try to help him relax. Donny didn't move. His eyes remained fixed on his hands. He hardly took a breath.

"It's okay, Donny. I'll even fill in the first comma for you. C'mon." Sadie smiled, trying to sound friendly.

Donny wiggled in his seat. His eyes darted from left to right. Everyone was watching him. His folded hands went down to his lap. He looked up at Sadie to see if she might look for someone else to call on.

Sadie began to worry that she had called on the wrong kid. She thought, "Oh boy, he's really nervous. I'll make it easy for him." In her kindest voice she said, "Here, Donny, take this marker and fill in just one punctuation mark."

Donny pressed his fists against the sides of his head, closed his eyes, and yelled, "WHY DON'T YOU LEAVE ME ALONE? WHY CAN'T YOU JUST LEAVE! ME! ALONE! YOU SHOULDN'T EVEN BE HERE. THIS IS MRS. GOLD-MAN'S CLASS."

Sadie took a half-step back as she stared at Donny.

"I HATE THIS!" he added. He turned his head toward the class. "AND DON'T STARE AT ME!" Suddenly he stood up. "I'M GOING HOME RIGHT NOW. I DON'T WANT TO

BE HERE." He began to walk to the door while his classmates sat motionless.

"Yikes! He's crazy!" Sadie thought as she dashed to the
door before Donny could reach it. She shot a look at the
others. Maybe someone could help, but they were glued
to their seats with very scared looks on their faces. Donny
approached the doorway. "Wait a minute, Donny. Take it
easy. You don't have to go to the whiteboard. You can just
watch from your seat if you'd like. I promise I won't call
on you again."

He stood in front of her and yelled at her, "LEAVE ME
ALONE AND GET OUT OF MY WAY! I DON'T WANT TO
BE HERE! THIS ISN'T RIGHT! I WANT TO GO HOME!"

Sadie put her arms out to block the door, but Donny
tried to push her aside. She pushed back to keep her
place. It looked like they might start wrestling. Sadie was
desperate. She lowered her voice and begged, "C'mon,
Donny. This will spoil the takeover day for the whole
school. Please don't go home! You won't have to do anything. I won't call on you anymore, I promise."

Donny stopped moving. He looked at her face, then
down at the floor. His face showed he was sad and confused. Sadie kept trying. "Mrs. Goldman will be proud
of you when she finds out that you did the schoolwork
today. She'll be proud of you that you were brave when
she wasn't here."

He looked at her again, and his face softened. Sadie
continued, "You're one of Mrs. Goldman's favorite students. She will be so proud of you. I really promise I won't

call on you for the rest of the day if you don't want me to, but just let's get through this day. It will all fall apart if you leave."

She paused. All was quiet for a moment. Then, "C'mon, Donny, please!" Her face slowly changed to a slight and pleading smile. The students remained motionless, holding their breaths.

Donny's body relaxed as his tight fists slowly began to open. He looked from Sadie to the other students. Some of them looked away. Finally he mumbled, "All right." He wiped his eyes and walked back to his desk with his head down. The students began to move again. The kid next to him reached over and patted him on the back, then whispered something to him. Donny flashed a quick smile, his first of the day.

Sadie quickly got someone else to fill in the missing punctuation. She wanted everything to get back to normal as soon as possible, so she gave the class a punctuation assignment at their desks. Donny did the work like everyone else. While they worked, Sadie jotted a note to Gil, which she would give to him at lunch.

Gil,

Donny Mueller had a meltdown. Almost went home. I talked him out of it. Just wanted to let you know.

Sadie

* * *

Mrs. Garcia slept late on her unexpected day off and then read the newspaper at breakfast. Later in the morning, she drove to Mr. Alston's house and rang his doorbell.

"Hello, Cindy, what a surprise!" said Mr. Alston. "What can I do for you?"

"Hi, Walter. Sorry to bother you, but I'd like to borrow your school key. I rushed out of my room yesterday, and I left my wallet there.

"Sure! Come on in, and I'll get the key for you."

"Thanks. Of all days to forget it . . . when I need it to do some shopping."

He peeled the key off his key ring and handed it to her. He said, "Cindy, don't you think it's risky leaving your wallet in the classroom? You never know who might spot it and take it."

"Not much chance of that, Walter. I stash it in an old cabinet under a messy pile of art supplies. No one ever looks in that cabinet for anything. I've been doing that for years. I don't use my handbag at school because I think it's an easy target for thieves."

"Well, all right. By the way, how are you doing with your class this year? I was angry with them after that incident with the Reese kid. And Mrs. Dower told me about a scuffle two boys had on the playground. They don't strike me as a very mature group."

"I've had some concerns also, Mr. Alston. There have been small problems with some of the boys and one of the girls, but lately the whole class has been very well-behaved."

"Is Priscilla Wright the girl you mean?"

"Yes. She's really all right, Mr. Alston. That incident with little PeeWee was an accident. She's not a problem student, although sometimes she's a little too pushy with her classmates. She also has very little patience for one certain classmate, but I think she's steady enough to grow out of it."

Mr. Alston asked, "How's the Glum girl doing? She had a rough time last year when her dad left. She became quiet and moody. Any changes?"

"Not so far. The students like her, but she keeps to herself. Lately I've noticed that she has been a little more involved, though. Dusty Rhodes seems to want to help her, and she lets him. I have heard that she says no to sleepover invitations and that she never invites anyone to her house. The girls leave her alone now."

"Well, keep an eye on her, and if you need me to help you with any of those kids, just let me know."

"Sure, Walter. I won't hesitate to ask."

The Teachers' Lounge

Gil and Dusty sat in the office at 11:40 A.M. They were feeling very good about how the day was going. Except for Alvin's accident in the gym, their takeover adventure was going well. Gil had taken a couple more observation walks around the school. All was going as planned. Dusty had the phones under control, and the mailman's and Mrs. Preston's visits were no real problem. Lunchtime was approaching, and a few classes were already arriving in the cafeteria.

Dusty said to Gil, "Guess where we eat lunch today?"

Gil smiled. "In the teachers' lounge."

"Yep! Let's go."

Leo called from the nurse's office, "I got the phones covered!"

The teachers' lounge was in the hallway between the school office and the cafeteria. Gil had never been in the teachers' lounge before, although he had peeked in many times. He knew that the teachers sat at tables with their salads and sandwiches. He had seen the bright red soda machine in there, something he had always wanted for the students. Of course, the principal always said no.

Mr. Alston told him he could get a soda at home or at a friend's house almost any time, but somehow a soda from the teachers' lounge seemed special.

When Gil and Dusty entered the lounge, some "teachers" were already there. Gil joked with them, "Oh, you came to lunch earlier than usual today!"

One of them said, "We couldn't wait! Hey, you guys, this is the best! This is awesome!" Dusty hooked a thumb under a suspender and said, "*Oooh!* I almost feel like a teacher."

Gil and Dusty turned their heads to quickly inspect the room. There were dishes lined up in a plastic drainer next to the sink. There were coffee mugs placed on a shelf with names written on some of them. The soda machine stood next to a white refrigerator. A microwave oven sat on a table close by. A coffee table that held magazines and a telephone was in front of the sofa at the end of the room. A gray copy machine the size of a small car sat in one corner, and next to it was a large worktable with papers, markers, scissors, and a humongous stapler.

The two boys joined the others at one of the tables and opened their lunch bags.

"They sure have a nice life in here, don't they, Gil?"

"Yeah, it's like home. Hey, anybody want a soda?"

"Sure," replied Dusty.

The two boys put money in the machine. They popped open the cans and clicked them together. Dusty made a toast. "Here's to the teachers at Central School!"

Why Me?

Just before lunchtime, Whitey and Phil checked out the cafeteria. They wanted to be sure that four chairs were around each table. The job was done in just a few minutes. Next, Whitey and another friend sat at a table for selling milk. As each class arrived, the students walked in a straight line right up to the milk table.

They walked with their milk and lunches to their tables and began eating. The room came alive with excited conversation. They were telling each other what happened in their classrooms during the morning. Bursts of laughter and raised voices bounced off the cafeteria walls.

For twenty more minutes, the rest of the classes filed in. In the fifth-grade section, Carl, Wes, and Duke sat together. As they began opening their lunch bags, they continued their discussion from class. Carl said, "Are you guys with me on this? I mean . . . about the fire alarm?"

Wes and Duke looked at each other to see what the other might say. They both hesitated. Carl began, "Don't worry, you guys. There's no problem. We won't get caught. There will be too much confusion. Maybe some kids will think it's a weather drill. We'll help out anyone who gets confused. Those hotshots in charge of the takeover will get totally busted. Hodges and his pals will be in deep trouble."

Duke and Wes nodded their heads. "Okay, Carl. Let's do it!" declared Duke.

"I've been thinking about this," said Carl. "Duke, I think you should pull the alarm."

Duke stopped chewing his sandwich and looked at Carl. Then he swallowed. "Wait a minute! Why me? This was your idea!"

"You are the smallest of us and the quickest. Your light green shirt blends in with the walls." Carl talked so fast that Duke couldn't get in a word. "You're on a bathroom break, you pull the alarm, then you walk quickly and calmly back into the room. No one sees you because the students are lining up in their rooms to go outside. Then we do our good deeds. Simple and smooth." Carl smiled, happy with himself for describing such a cool idea.

Duke looked at Wes. He was quite uncertain.

"You can do it!" Wes encouraged him.

"Oh, thanks a lot!" Duke glared at Wes, then turned back to Carl. He felt outnumbered. Meekly he said, "Okay."

Carl got excited and leaned forward with new enthusiasm. "As the classrooms empty, we keep an eye out for anyone who is crying or scared. We help them out by telling them "no talking, no running," and where to go. We're the last ones to leave the building. We'll be heroes, I'm telling you."

Carl held up his hand for a high five. All three of them slapped hands, then continued talking and eating. Before they left the cafeteria, Carl told Duke, "You should do it soon after lunch."

Mimics

After Sarah dropped off her students at the cafeteria door, she turned to walk toward the teachers' lounge. She saw Priscilla down the hallway about to enter the lounge. Their eyes met. Sarah built up her courage and called out to her, "Priscilla, hi!" She waved a hand.

Priscilla looked up, surprised that Sarah had spoken to her. Sarah smiled, but Priscilla flashed an impatient look and turned to walk through the doorway. Sarah's smile faded into a blank stare. Some tears came to her eyes. She stood for a moment, then moved slowly toward the teachers' lounge.

Moments before, when Priscilla entered the lounge, her impatient look changed instantly to a bright smile. She scanned the whole room and everyone in it and said, "Well, la-dee-da, we're in the famous teachers' lounge. *Wooo wooo!* Let's have a party. It's the only chance we'll ever get!" Everyone laughed.

Priscilla raised her arms and began a silly dance around the room. Everyone watched her as she sang "Twinkle Twinkle Little Star" in a falsetto voice, while she touched everything she danced by. She turned the sink faucet on and off. She read the notes on the bulletin board. "Oh listen, everybody! Report card grades must be completed by November 14." She turned and pointed to Kelly. "Give Priscilla all As." She danced her way to the refrigerator and opened the door. "Oh look!" she said. "A carton of milk and some old lunch bags. What nice grease stains they have!" More laughing.

Sarah slipped quietly into the teachers' lounge during Priscilla's musical act and walked to an empty table. She sat down and opened her lunch bag.

Priscilla had closed the refrigerator door and glided gracefully to the microwave. She set it at four seconds and pushed the start button. It hummed a beeping sound. She moved to the copy machine and raised the lid, placed her hand on the glass, lowered the lid, and pushed the start button. The machine whined, a green light slid under her hand, and a sheet of paper squeezed out the side. She held the paper up for all to see. It showed a black image of her hand with fingers spread apart. Everyone laughed, and Priscilla tacked it to the bulletin board. She finally sat down after Whitey and Phil came in.

Minutes later Bobby arrived. He stopped at the doorway and spoke loudly to an imaginary person. "Mrs. Dower, you have been very naughty today, beating up first graders and spitting in the hallway. You, my dear, are fired! Please bend over for a spanking!" Everyone laughed as Bobby acted out the spanking.

Kelly burst in with arms opened wide and announced, "I now declare that school is closed! You may all go home!" Cheers.

Eventually they settled down and everyone started sharing their morning stories. Priscilla said, "I was so afraid that a mother would insist on coming into the classroom with her child, looking for Miss Melody." She changed her voice to almost a song. "But I was so cool. I told them Miss Melody was letting us have the little ones come in on their own. We were trying to build responsible students."

Then her tone turned serious. "That's when I whispered to the kids that cookies were on the table in the classroom. 'Go ahead in and help yourself,' I told them. They almost ran into the room. Kindergarten is the best!"

Kelly cut in. "I was really nervous at the beginning too. I had a stomachache for the first hour. Carl and his buddies were mad that they weren't included in our secret, so I told them to look you up, Gil."

Gil said, "Uh oh! I forgot all about Carl. I hope he doesn't mess this up."

Sadie began to tell her morning tale. "You think you had problems. You guys know Donny Mueller?"

"Oh yeah, he's the big one in fourth grade," said Bobby.

"He spazzed out this morning when I called on him. He yelled and screamed and then tried to leave. Said he wanted to go home." Sadie pulled a note out of her pocket and passed it to Gil. "I forgot that I wrote you a note about it."

He read the note, then asked, "What did you do, Sadie?"

"I blocked the door and talked fast. I can't even remember what I said. I was just so scared that he was going to go home. I pleaded with him, and he finally settled down."

Sarah, still sitting alone at a table, suddenly sat up straight and took a breath. "I almost blew it too." All heads turned to face her with surprised looks. It was the first time they had heard her join a group discussion in almost a year.

Sarah continued, "I started off really strict, but the kids were talking and not doing what I said." She skipped the part where she cried. "One of the girls told me that if I would be nicer, the class probably would behave better." She smiled. "And it worked!"

Phil spoke up. "Good job, Sarah."

"Yeah, nice work, Sarah," said Sadie. "Hey, don't sit over there all alone. C'mere and join us." Sarah gathered up her sandwich and napkin. Sadie and the other girls greeted her. Priscilla sat quietly eating a sandwich.

They quickly went back to sharing their morning stories. Phil described climbing through the bars in front of the window. Dusty told them about some of the phone calls he took in the office, and Gil talked about the mailman and Mrs. Preston. A first-grade "teacher," Dylan Hunt, shared a story about one of his boys using a black marker to put lines on his cheeks right under his eyes. "I asked him why he did that, and he answered, 'So I look like a quarterback.'"

Phil spoke up again. He changed to a lower voice. "Okay, boys and girls, jog two laps around the gym, no passing, no touching, no whining!"

Bobby responded, "Hey, you sound just like Mr. Mays!"

Phil stood up and said, "Okay, who's this?" He changed his expression to look gentle and sweet and said, "Now I know you two are having a disagreement, but fighting isn't the answer."

"Mrs. Garcia!" shouted Dusty.

"I got one," said Priscilla. She stood up and began pacing back and forth, then spoke in a low voice. "You will not be a happy camper if your paper is not turned in on time." Three people yelled at the same time, "Mrs. Goldman!"

"Okay, who's this?" Bobby looked around at everyone and raised his eyebrows as high as he could.

"Stoney," yelled four of his friends.

Whitey announced, "This is the best lunch period we ever had." They continued eating, talking, and laughing. A few minutes later, Melissa Burton burst through the door with enough force to knock it down. She looked terrified as she yelled, "Where's Gil?"

Gil shot to his feet and said, "Here I am. What happened now?"

Melissa shot back, "Mrs. Garcia is here!"

Silver-dollar Eyes

When Phil was in the lounge telling about climbing through the barred window, Mrs. Garcia was parking her car down the street from the school. She had complained for years about the school not having its own parking lot. As usual, nothing was done about it.

"I wonder where the plumbers are," she thought. "They're probably eating lunch back on the playground."

She walked to the front door and unlocked it. "I'll just slip in, grab my wallet, and slip out before they even know I'm here."

Leo was sitting at the secretary's desk, his head buried in the first-aid book. He didn't see Mrs. Garcia come in, and she didn't see Leo as she rushed by the office. Then she heard children's voices coming from the cafeteria. "Strange! Maybe Girl Scouts? No, not during school hours. I'll just take a quick look."

Melissa was standing near the cafeteria entrance, holding a damp rag. Mrs. Garcia walked up alongside her, stopped, and stared at all the students. Melissa turned slightly, and when she saw her teacher's wide-open mouth, she jumped three inches off the floor. "Oh, Mrs. Garcia!" she yelled.

Mrs. Garcia's eyes were as big as silver dollars.

"Uh . . . uh . . . Mrs. Garcia, what are you doing here?"

Mrs. Garcia looked directly at her student. "Melissa, the question is, what are you doing here? I thought there was no school today. Why are all these children here?" Mrs. Garcia didn't wait for an answer. She spun around and walked toward the office. Melissa ran past her, looking over her shoulder. She shouted, "I'll tell Gil you're here."

"Gil? Gil Hodges?" Mrs. Garcia's voice was two pitches higher than normal. "What's going on here?"

"I'll get Gil. He'll explain everything," she said as she slammed open the door of the teachers' lounge.

* * *

Melissa held the door open and yelled to Gil, "Mrs. Garcia is here. She's already been to the cafeteria, and now she's coming up the hallway! I told her I would get you."

Everyone looked at Gil. They knew that their special day was over. Gil rushed out through the door and bumped into Mrs. Garcia in the hallway. "Ow!" yelled his teacher. She steadied herself and said, "Gil, what's happening? Why are all these children here?"

"Uh, hi, Mrs. Garcia. Uh, okay, I'll tell you what's happening. Come into my office. I'll tell you everything, I promise."

"Your office? Oh yes, Gil, you had better tell me everything!" she barked. "Does Mr. Alston know you're here?"

"Um, no." They entered the main office and Leo saw them turn into Mr. Alston's smaller office. Leo hid his head in his book. Gil sat in the principal's desk chair. He pointed to a visitor's chair and said, "Please, sit."

She glared at him, and when he shrugged his shoulders she plopped down and crossed her arms in front of her. Gil sat back in the huge chair. He thought quickly. He and his friends were already in big trouble. Lying would only make it worse. Besides, he couldn't think of a lie that could possibly save them. So he started, "Remember when Priscilla knocked over PeeWee Reese last week, and Mr. Alston took away Catch One–Catch All?"

"Yes, I remember." Her eyes were squarely aimed at Gil's, as if she were saying, "Yes, yes, keep talking!"

Gil explained the point they wanted to make to Mr. Alston. "We want him to know we can handle big jobs. One mistake doesn't mean we aren't able to do good things and handle problems." He hesitated. Then he raised his hands chest high, palms up, and continued, "We're running the school. It's going well." Mrs. Garcia's mouth dropped open again. Gil added, "Today, fifth graders are the teachers, and the students are learning."

Mrs. Garcia closed her mouth, looked up at the ceiling, put her hand to her forehead, and said, "What! I don't believe this!" She looked back at Gil. "How did you do it? How did you get in?"

He told her the whole story, from the planning to the actual day. He left nothing out. He felt that if he were completely honest with her, she might give him some credit for that and not be so mad.

Mrs. Garcia said, "And I thought you were all working so hard on schoolwork. Ugh! And those long trips to the washroom! Now I get it!" She shook her head and exclaimed, "Ha! You sure snookered me."

"Please don't give us away, Mrs. Garcia. It's going really good."

"It's going really *well*," she corrected.

"The teachers are all doing a good job, and every classroom is running smoothly," he continued. "I've checked. The school day has been normal, and we want to be able to finish it."

"Oh, Gil, I don't know what to do. Now that I know what's going on I can't just go home as if nothing has happened."

"Why not? It's working."

"Well, teachers are instructed never to leave students alone anywhere at school without an adult present. It's a legal matter. And right now I can't walk out of here knowing my school is full of children with no adult supervision. If Mr. Alston discovered that I knew about this and didn't tell him, he'd fire me just like that." She snapped her fingers. "And I wouldn't blame him."

Gil frowned.

She added, "If someone got hurt, I would never forgive myself."

He understood her problem. "I don't want you to get fired, and I don't want anyone to get hurt, Mrs. Garcia, but I don't want to quit either. You saw how well the kids were behaving in the cafeteria. Please don't make us stop."

The teacher stared at Gil and said, "I don't know, Gil. I don't think there's any way out of this."

They sat quietly for a moment.

"Here's an idea," said Gil. "How about you give me your phone number and then go home. If anything happens, we will call you immediately, and you can come back right away."

Mrs. Garcia didn't hesitate. "Can't do it! Too much time would pass before I could get here if there were an emergency. Besides, once I leave this building I'm fired. I know it!" She was slowly shaking her head as she finished.

They sat in silence again. Mrs. Garcia watched him stare off into space, looking for a miracle.

"Wait!" Gil said. "Here's an idea."

Her voice was impatient. "What?"

"How about if you stay in the building but keep out of sight, like, in the conference room. We finish out the day, but if something bad happens and we need you, you're already here."

Mrs. Garcia scrunched her forehead as she thought about it. "Hmm. That has possibilities, Gil. You would have to absolutely promise me that you would come and get me immediately if there were an emergency, something that you couldn't handle."

"Yes, I promise."

Mrs. Garcia thought aloud. "I could go to the conference room now, while everyone is in the cafeteria. Most of the students don't know I'm here." She looked up at Gil. "You should tell those who do know I'm here not to tell anyone else. It would not be good for everyone to know. I think this might work."

Gil frowned. He was glad that she liked the idea, but he didn't really want an adult in the school. He wanted to be able to say that the students did it without adult help, but he also knew that this plan was the only way Mrs. Garcia would allow them to continue.

"Okay!" he exclaimed. "Let's do that. You stay in the conference room. Thank you so much, Mrs. Garcia. I know you're taking a big chance, and we really appreciate what you are doing for us. We won't let you down, I promise."

Mrs. Garcia said, "You are welcome, Gil. Remember that I am counting on you."

She stood up smiling and shook Gil's hand. She looked both ways outside the office door. "Okay, I'm going to the conference room now." As she stepped into the hallway, Gil heard her mutter to herself, "I can't believe I'm doing this."

"Thanks for not squealing on us, Mrs. Garcia!" he smiled. She turned, winked, then walked quickly toward the conference room.

When Gil walked back to the lounge, his friends pounced on him with questions. "What happened? Are we busted? My parents are going to kill me!"

"It's okay." Gil said. He motioned with his hands to settle down. "Mrs. Garcia is letting us continue, but she's staying in the school. She said she'd get fired if she left us here without any adults. She made me promise to let her know if there's an emergency we can't handle." He continued, "Don't tell anyone that she's here because she'll get in big trouble if that gets out. She wants us to succeed at this, but she doesn't want anything bad to happen. We just keep doing what we've been doing and hope the afternoon goes well."

"She's letting us stay?" said Dusty. "Mrs. Garcia is awesome!"

"She sure is," said Sadie. "She could bust us. Why'd she come to school in the first place?"

Gil answered, "Something about leaving her wallet here yesterday." Gil changed his tone. "She's giving us a break. We're really lucky it was Mrs. Garcia who showed up and not you-know-who."

"Yeah," said Sadie. "Mrs. Dower would have called the police on us."

Gil changed his nervous voice to his in-charge voice. "Okay, lunch recess ends in fifteen minutes. Hang out in here till the bell rings. Keep everything going smoothly this afternoon, right to the end, okay? We don't want to have to go to Mrs. Garcia for help."

They went back to finishing their lunches. Gil picked up some magazines from the teachers' lounge and brought them to the conference room. He tapped lightly on the door. When Mrs. Garcia opened it a crack, he handed the magazines to her.

"Thanks!" she said in a low voice. "See you at the end of the day." She smiled and held up her crossed fingers as he closed the door. Gil returned to the cafeteria to tell Melissa to keep Mrs. Garcia's visit a total secret. He then returned to the office to give Leo a break and let him get some lunch with his friends.

Mrs. Garcia stood at the conference room door for a moment, thinking, "I must be crazy. They're just kids. Oh brother! I hope I have a job on Monday."

The Old Smell

At about ten thirty that same Friday morning Hank Thompson was applying a little more polish onto his motorcycle. He was thinking about how long it had been since he'd had any money in his pockets. He hated being broke, but he had a plan.

"I've been watching that school for weeks. It should be an easy job."

He rubbed the polish harder against the gas tank of his motorcycle. Suddenly he threw the rag down and said out loud, "I gotta do it today. If I don't do it today, I'll never do it."

He had been taking walks along Fourth and Academy Streets for weeks, studying the movements of students and teachers at lunchtime. He learned when the bells rang, when students were in the schoolyard, and when classes were outside at recess. He had figured out what the best time of day would be to enter the school without being noticed.

Things hadn't been going well for Hank since high school. He'd been arrested for misdemeanor burglary and fighting. It had been difficult for him to keep any job for more than a month. His bosses told him he had a bad temper. They had all these stupid rules about being on time and working nights and Saturdays. His girlfriend nagged him about wearing nicer clothes and not drinking so much. "I've just been a little unlucky," he thought. "All I need is a break or two."

He remembered how much he hated school. He couldn't remember having even one good day there—too much homework, walking in lines, not talking during class.

Home wasn't much better. His parents had their own rules when he was growing up: what to eat, what not to eat, when to eat, which TV shows he couldn't watch, what time he had to be home. He had no freedom. His folks were out as much as they were home. They worked in the city and were busy, busy, busy. His mom usually phoned home around five o'clock.

"Hello!"

"Hi, Hank, it's Mom. Dad and I are still downtown and won't be home for a while. Fix yourself a turkey sandwich. There's ham in the fridge too. Bye, Hon."

Hank made his own choices when he was alone. He ate what and when he wanted. He knew every show that was on TV and was really good at computer games like "Army Killer" and "High School Bully." He made some friends during his school days, but when he hung out with them it usually ended up with arguments.

Hank was good at noticing details that others missed. He saw teachers sneaking snacks from their desk drawers. He knew which of his classmates cheated on tests, and he noticed which kids wore the same clothes every day. He also observed that at lunchtime the teachers left their rooms unlocked when they went to the teachers' lounge. He remembered that their handbags were left hanging over the backs of their chairs while they were gone.

Hank made his move during the lunch recess at Central School. He was unaware that only children were in the teachers' lounge. While he was walking toward the school, he also didn't know that there was a student sitting at the principal's desk talking to a very surprised teacher. A little later, while the cafeteria and playground were crowded with students, Hank snuck in through the same fourth-grade doorway that the "teachers" entered that morning. He knew that door would be unlocked. He had seen teachers coming and going for lunches when he was checking out the school earlier.

No one saw him as he entered the school. He looked up and down both hallways, then dashed into the boys' washroom. "Okay! So far, so good," he said to himself.

His breathing was faster than normal. He looked in the same mirror that was there seventeen years earlier. His hair was messy. The whiskers on his face made him look older than twenty. His blue jeans were grease-stained. His sweatshirt was dirty around the collar. He didn't have that look on his face that teachers described as "attitude;" he was nervous and excited at the same time.

He glanced at his watch. He knew from his walks what time everyone would be back in the building. "I've got twenty minutes. I'll be done in ten," he told himself.

The Old Smell

Hank peeked out the door of the washroom and looked both ways. The school building hadn't changed much since when he was a student. To the right, he saw the office, the main entrance, and some classrooms. On his left was a hallway with more classrooms.

"I'll be happy with just one wallet," he said to himself.

He hurried down the hallway to the farthest classroom from the office. It was his old fifth-grade classroom. Mrs. Garcia's name was on the door. His eyes went right to her chair. No handbag! "What?"

He looked around the room for another place where the teacher might leave her purse. "I don't remember the room being this small." He saw six computers along a wall, and the students' desks were arranged in groups of four.

"*Humph!* We had to sit in rows."

The walls were light blue, not the light yellow he remembered. One thing was still the same, though. That smell! Schools all have that smell. Is it the paper? The floor wax? Suddenly his stomach felt strange. He forced himself out of those old memories and rushed to the teacher's desk. He opened and closed every drawer rapidly. There was nothing there but pens, paper clips, and other useless articles. He searched the teacher's coat closet—nothing but hangers and old, rolled-up wall maps leaning against the wall. He looked inside an old cabinet that had piles of art paper and other art supplies. He nervously picked through some of the art paper, but he quit searching when he saw so many piles. There was no handbag, no wallet, no money.

"Nothing here? This is crazy." He rushed to the door and shot a look down the hallway. Empty. He bolted out and ran on tiptoes into the next classroom.

While he began slamming drawers in the second room, Mrs. Garcia was reading a magazine in the conference room. Outside, the playground was loud with kids shouting and playing. Some of the fifth graders were finishing up their lunches in the teachers' lounge.

It's Turning Out to Be All Right

If people were looking down at the playground from a blimp, it would look like a colony of ants. Tiny figures of kids were walking and running in all directions. On the grassy field, small images of boys and girls were chasing after a tiny soccer ball. On the blacktop, a kickball was flying into the air, and a kid was running along a white line toward first base. A jump rope looped in circles and slapped the ground. Some kids were standing alone; others were in small groups. Two fifth graders watched over the games like regular recess supervisors.

Donny was there, standing alone. He settled down after his problem with Sadie and those dumb punctuation marks. When he had first realized that no adults would be at school, he was afraid that bullies would bother him and that the classroom would be loud. But it had been a quiet morning, and he felt better now. He was glad it was recess time, even though he didn't usually get involved in group games. He wasn't very good at sports, but he was a fast runner for a kid his size and stronger than most. Occasionally he would get into a game of tag, but he didn't feel like it today. Today he just stood and watched, keeping his hands in his pockets.

"Hey, Donny, wanna play kickball?" yelled a classmate. Donny, startled when he heard his name, jerked his hands up. He knew they were trying to be nice to him, but he felt safer just watching. He shook his head no at the invitation and walked a few steps away. "I think I'll go inside," he said to himself. "No one's there. I'll just wait for everyone in our room."

Donny strolled toward the fourth-grade entrance with his hands back in his pockets. No one noticed him leaving the playground. He walked right into his classroom. Relieved to be alone, he plopped down at his desk and relaxed. He was feeling good. "This day is turning out to be all right." He was glad he stayed at school.

Right after he sat down, however, he heard desk drawers opening and closing in a room right down the hall. Someone was in a classroom. He stood up and walked to the hallway to see who it was.

The Plunger

Hank stared at the empty teacher's chair. "No handbag here either! What's going on with these teachers? Don't they pay them?"

He searched the entire room. Nothing. He opened and closed every desk drawer. In frustration he closed the last one extra hard. "I can't believe it!" he exclaimed. "I'm not leaving this place empty-handed!"

He shot a quick look at the wall clock. "Still almost fifteen minutes before the bell!"

Hank rushed to the door, and as he turned toward the fourth-grade room he yelled, "Oh!" Five feet in front of him, frozen in terror, was a rather large student.

"Who are you?" asked Donny in a very shaky voice. The stranger stared at him, looking confused. The boy knew that this guy was definitely not someone who should be in that classroom. Donny turned and ran. The stranger bolted after him and grabbed him by the shirt collar. He pulled him back, hard enough to raise the boy's feet off the floor.

"*Ahhh!*" Donny screamed. He slid four feet on his back along the glossy tile floor.

The angry man tried quickly to grab the kid again. Without thinking, Donny shot back on his feet and raced into the washroom. He hurried to the farthest wall, turned around, and pressed his back against the cold tile. The washroom door flew open and smacked the wall. The stranger appeared, his face twisted in anger. He stared hard at Donny. The frightened student pressed himself harder against the tile. A weak "*Uhh*" came from his throat.

"*Shhh!*" motioned the man. He wasn't sure what to do, and he felt bad about grabbing and throwing the boy. He looked down and shook his head, like he was trying to think clearly.

Donny was as still as a statue as he watched the man's face. His arms were at his sides, his hands flat against the tile. His leg was pressed against an empty water bucket on one side. The dull-green toilet stalls were on Donny's left. In the pail was a toilet plunger that had a black suction cup connected to the end of a wooden handle.

"Stay away from me!" he shouted. His eyes were scrunched up tight enough to make wrinkles across his forehead. "Go away!" he commanded. He continued to stare at the man's face.

"*Shhh!* Hey, kid, I'm just visiting. I used to go here. I'm not gonna hurt ya."

Donny heard the man's voice echo off the washroom walls. "Leave me alone! Get out of here!"

Hank knew he had less than ten minutes to quiet this kid, grab a wallet from a classroom, and get out of the school. He took a step closer to Donny. "Really, kid, I just need for you to be quiet. I just want to look around a little. *Shhh.*"

Donny yelled, "Go away." He started to cry softly. Hank reached for Donny and tried to cup his hand over Donny's mouth. Donny grabbed at the handle of the plunger, and with one movement he swung it wildly at the man. The blow smacked Hank just over his left ear. It would have been a home run in a ballpark.

Hank's knees bent a little. "Ow!" He covered his head with both hands and raged in anger. "You ugly little twerp!"

Donny saw that he had hurt the stranger, but he knew he was still dangerous. Then he did what his parents told him to do if he was ever cornered by a bad guy. He stepped forward, and with great force he kicked the man squarely between his legs.

"*Owwooooeee!*" Hank sounded like a wounded bear. He dropped to his knees and then fell to the floor. He lay on his side, holding his middle section with both hands. His yells weakened into grunts. "Uh. Uh. Uh. . . ."

Donny, still big-eyed and short-breathed, ran to the door, flung it open as hard as he could, and took off running in the hallway screaming, "Help! Help! I just beat up a bad guy!"

Leo came running out of the office. "Hey! What happened?"

Donny never stopped running. He barked over his shoulder, "There's a dirty, hairy man lying on the floor in the bathroom. He tried to grab me, so I kicked him a good one." He pointed in the direction of the washroom.

Leo froze. "A dirty, hairy man? No way am I going into that washroom without six other guys." He followed Donny down the hallway.

The fifth graders in the teachers' lounge were still laughing as they finished their lunches and started to return to their rooms. When Whitey opened the teachers' lounge door into the hallway, Donny crashed into him. He yelled, "There's a man in the washroom!" he bellowed. "He tried to grab me. I kicked him where it hurts, and he's down on the floor!"

The fifth graders, in total shock, stood and stared. Who is this kid? "What?" cried out Priscilla.

He shouted again, "C'mon! Come with me! Hurry!" He turned and waved his arm in quick circles. They hesitated, looking very confused. "I hurt him pretty bad! He's down. He's hurt!" He waved his arm more rapidly. "C'mon!" he insisted.

Gil and five others tore after Donny at full speed. They stopped at the washroom door. "He's in there," Donny whispered in an excited voice. Gil opened the door a couple of inches and snuck a look. The others bunched close behind, standing on tiptoes and peering over his shoulder. The man was still lying on his side on the washroom floor, facing away from them. They saw a little of the side of his face, enough to notice the gash between his ear and eye. He was moaning, and there was vomit on the floor near his head. He was making grunting noises. *"Uh! Uh!"* He wasn't trying to get up. His hands were still folded over his lap.

Gil and the others backed into the hallway. Gil spoke quietly, "If we report him, the takeover is done. If we leave him in there, he could hurt someone. The classes are coming inside soon."

"Let's tie him up while he's still in bad shape," said Gil.

"With what?" asked Bobby.

Whitey said. "There's duct tape in the custodian's office."

"Good," snapped Gil. "Get it! Fast!"

Whitey took off running. They could still hear grunts coming from the washroom.

"I don't want anyone to know he's here. They'll get scared. We have to hide him where no one will see him."

Phil said, "In the basement! It's perfect! With the door closed, no one would hear him even if he yells."

"Good!" Gil responded. "Let's tape him up good and drag him down there." He looked around nervously. "Where's Whitey? We've got to hurry before this guy recovers." Gil looked inside again. The man was on his knees.

Gil gasped sharply. "I know him," he exclaimed. "It's the motorcycle guy. He's my neighbor. He lives in the house behind my backyard. I don't know him that well, but he seemed like a good guy." He looked for Whitey, then turned to Dusty. Give me your suspenders, fast!" He turned to the others. "We need to tie him down now."

Dusty unhooked his suspenders and passed them to Gil. "Everyone, jump on him and keep him down. Let's go!" whispered Gil. They rushed in and pounced on

Hank. Some landed on his chest and stomach; others pinned down his arms and legs. Donny landed across his chest. *"Offf!"* Hank grunted as the air was squeezed out from his lungs.

Hank's eyes were half open as he lay pinned on his back. Gil wrapped his legs together with two suspender strands. He whispered into his ear, "Sorry, Hank. I gotta do this." He said to the others, "Press his hands together." They forced Hank's hands together like he was praying. Gil wrapped his wrists tightly with the other two suspender strands, making triple knots, and pulled them tight.

"Dusty, go get the scissors from the office."

Dusty took off for the office. The students continued to hold down their prisoner as they waited for Whitey. Phil added to the problem by saying, "Yuck! It smells like throw-up in here."

Bobby agreed. "It's disgusting," and quickly changed the subject. "Hey, Donny, what did you do to him?"

Donny answered. "I just whacked him in the head and kicked him where it counts."

"Wow," said Bobby with a big grin. "You are an animal!" The others smiled at Donny. He smiled back. Suddenly the door exploded open with another loud crack against the wall. Whitey rushed in at full speed and slapped a roll of gray tape into Gil's hand.

Gil said, "All right! Here's what we do. I'll tape his feet together; then you guys grab his arms so I can tape his wrists."

Hank was beginning to be more alert. His eyes were clearer, but he didn't resist while Gil wrapped circles of tape over the suspenders.

"Ow!" he wheezed. Suddenly Hank was totally clear-headed. He looked around at all the faces. He noticed Gil and mumbled, "Hey, I know you."

"Hi, Hank," said Gil. "I'm not sure what you're doing here or why you grabbed this kid, but you're going to have to stay with us for a while." Hank slowly shook his head back and forth, like he was totally confused. Donny rolled off him, picked up the plunger, and cocked it, ready to smack him again.

Hank screamed, "Keep that kid away from me."

Gil ignored his neighbor. "Bobby, Priscilla, grab his feet! Let's get him out of here!" They dragged the helpless intruder feet first. He slid along the floor on his back. Donny followed behind them, holding the plunger near Hank's head. Dusty followed, holding up his pants as he walked. Hank silently watched the ceiling go by as he was being dragged down the hallway. They got to the basement door quickly.

At the top of the stairs, Bobby looked down the fourteen steps. He said, "We could roll him down."

"*Nooo!*" moaned Hank.

Dusty said, "Let's pull him down head first. Grab his shoulders. Hurry, the bell is going to ring."

Dusty and Gil grabbed Hank's shirt and shoulders. Dusty said, "Bobby, c'mon over here and grab his shoulder."

They spun him around at the top of the stairway and pulled him down through the doorway. The man's feet banged on each step as they descended. "Don't drop me!" he choked. Donny still followed with the plunger. Hank flopped onto the cold concrete floor. *"Ahhh! Easy!"* he shouted.

Dusty spotted a huge pipe near the far wall. It ran from the ceiling to the floor. He let go of his pants with one hand and pointed with the other. "Over there," he directed.

Gil and Bobby dragged Hank to the pipe and sat him up with his back against it. As they held his arms up, Whitey wrapped the tape around Hank's chest and lashed him to the pipe. "Go around three or four times and keep it tight," instructed Bobby. When they finished, Hank was sitting upright, taped to the pipe. His wrists and ankles were also tightly wrapped. Dusty grabbed the role of tape and said, "I'll keep this on my desk, just in case we need it again."

Gil responded, "Okay, Dusty." He turned to Hank and said, "What were you doing in our school?"

Hank waited a moment and said, "Just checking out what the old school looked like."

Whitey spat out, "Oh, sure, right!"

Gil interrupted. "We're going to leave you here until school is out. If you make any noise down here, we will have to tape your mouth closed." Whitey stepped in and put his face close to Hank's. He warned, "You don't want that."

The Plunger

Hank shook his head back and forth. All of them walked up the basement stairs, leaving Hank sitting on the dirty, cool basement floor. His stomach was still upset, his head hurt, and his groin ached.

She Pressed
Three Numbers

About forty-five minutes earlier, before Hank was tied up in the boys' bathroom, Mrs. Teller had walked to Central School to pick up her daughter for lunch at their favorite restaurant. She saw a young man that she recognized from the neighborhood walking near her. "Good morning," she said with a big smile. "I usually see you riding your beautiful motorcycle. It's good to see you walking."

He answered, "Oh, yeah. I thought I'd leave my motorcycle home today and take a walk in the neighborhood." He turned to cross the street. "Have a good day."

She answered, "Thanks, you too." She thought, "He lives somewhere around here. Hmm! He would be a handsome young man if he would just clean himself up a little."

Jessica Teller met her mother on the sidewalk outside the school. "Look at my new cat puppet, Mommy! I named her Midnight."

"Wow, Sweetheart! She's beautiful!"

"Mom, we had so much fun today."

Mrs. Teller smiled down at her daughter, happy to see her so excited. They held hands and began their walk.

"We cut out cats and colored them. We painted, and we got to play for a long time in the play kitchen. We had a lot of snacks like pretzels and raisins and cookies and juice. It was the best morning!"

"Wow! You sure did a lot today, Jess. I'm glad you had a good day."

"Mommy, my teacher was a fifth grader. Her name is Priscilla."

"Oh really? Her mother was amused. "Where was Miss Melody?"

"I don't know. I didn't see her today. Priscilla and some others were helping the teachers."

"Oh really!" her mom repeated, sounding more interested.

"I hope Priscilla teaches us again some time. She was fun."

Jessica's mom flashed a big smile. "Hey, Jessica, what do you say we go to the Savory Sandwich Center for lunch today?"

"Oh goody, Mommy. I want peanut butter and jelly on pita bread."

Her mom laughed.

* * *

While Jessica and her mother were finishing their sandwiches, her mom said, "Jess, I need to make a phone call. It's private. I'll be right back."

"Okay."

Mrs. Teller walked to a corner of the restaurant where there was a pay phone hanging on the wall. "Hello, Margaret, this is Jean. Did Jennie say anything to you about Miss Melody not being in class today?"

"No," answered her friend, "but wait, she's right here. Hang on a minute." Mrs. Teller heard muffled voices, then Jennie's mom returned to the phone. Her voice had turned serious.

"Jean, Jennie said a student took Miss Melody's place. And boy, did Jennie ever love school today! She's been talking nonstop about all the fun she had."

"Really? Margaret, I think something's up at the school. I'll call you back later. Bye bye!"

＊ ＊ ＊

Leo liked taking phone calls in the office. The next time the phone rang he answered it on the first ring. "Central School. May I help you?"

Pause.

"He's not in right now, may I take a message?" Leo listened quietly for a half-minute.

"Oh no, Mrs. Teller, there's no problem. The teacher just let a fifth grader lead the activities this morning. She likes to let older students do special projects." Leo thought it might be a good idea to explain why. "She says that sometimes it's a good idea to let children teach children. It keeps things interesting."

After another pause, he answered, "No, not very often." Pause.

"Oh yes, it's only for one day."

Pause. "You're welcome."

Leo thought he should tell Gill and Dusty about the call after lunch.

Mrs. Teller hung up. "Hmm! No secretary either." She looked at her phone again and pressed three numbers.

*   *   *

Fifth graders Chris and Lauren strolled around the playground together, talking as they supervised the students at recess. They liked being in charge. They felt important as they watched over the safety of the students. Suddenly a young boy approached them and complained, "Michael keeps teasing me about my haircut."

"What's your name?" asked Lauren.

"Peter," said the teary-eyed boy.

"What grade are you in?"

"First."

"Show me who Michael is," Lauren said in her teacher voice. Peter pointed, and they walked over to Michael. He was playing tag with his buddies.

"Hey, Michael!" shouted Lauren. She waved for Michael to approach her. He walked over and said, "Am I in trouble?"

Lauren said, "Peter is not happy that you teased him about his hair."

Michael looked at Peter. "Sorry," he said.

"Will you promise that you won't tease him anymore?"

Michael put on a sad face. He looked at Peter again and said, "Sorry, I won't do it again." Both boys ran off and joined the game of tag.

A police car rolled into view of the playground at the same time that Hank was being tied up in the school basement. Officer Larkin was performing his usual patrol of the neighborhoods when he received a radio message to check out Central School. Some lady had called the police station and asked them to take a look. Officer Larkin drove slowly by the playground. He said to himself, "Man, these kids sure have a lot of energy. Look at them running all over the place!"

As he inched his black squad car past the playground everything looked as it always did. "These kids look fine. No one is hurt. It's like every other day,"

He parked at the curb and watched for five minutes. "I guess it's all fine. Walt Alston is an old friend of mine. I'll just stop in and say hello, just to be sure. As he stepped onto the walkway that led to the front door, he heard a lady's voice calling. "Pete! Pete!" He looked around to see Mrs. Preston waving to him from across the street. "Got a minute?"

The officer shouted back, "Good morning, Mary. Sure!" He turned and hustled over to talk with the PTA president.

"How are you?" the officer asked.

"Fine, Pete, how about yourself?"

"Very well, thank you."

"Have you got police business inside Central School?"

"I guess you could say that. We got a call from a lady asking us to check to see that everything is okay. I'm on my way in to see Walt."

"It's fine over there, Pete. I was in there earlier today. Some of the older kids are helping out the secretary and some teachers by working with the younger kids. That's all. I'm an old PTA mom who's been in and out of that school for fifteen years, and I'd sure know if something was wrong. By the way, I'll be needing the bicycle safety booklets very soon."

"You're in luck, Mary. I just happen to have them in my squad car."

"Wonderful! May I have them?" she asked.

"Of course you can." They walked over to the car, and he gave Mrs. Preston the small booklets. Suddenly his police radio came to life. "Twenty-seven!" was all it said.

The officer grabbed the radio from his waist. "Twenty-seven!" he answered.

The woman's voice on the speaker was calm and quick. "Auto accident on Prospect Street and Roland. May be injuries. Can you take it?"

The police officer looked at his friend, then at the school. Mrs. Preston waved her hand slightly and said, "Oh, it's fine in there, Pete."

He held the radio to his mouth and said, "Affirmative! On my way. Ten-four! "

Mrs. Preston waved good-bye as Officer Larkin hurried to his car. "Bye, Mary. See you later." He sped off with lights flashing and siren blaring. Mrs. Preston walked back to her home. She glanced over her shoulder at the playground and saw that the children were playing as usual. "Oh, of course it's fine."

Hank, who was wiggling and twisting on the basement floor, was planning his escape.

Tents, Muscles, and Toiletries

When the Central School bell sounded to end lunch recess, the students squeezed through doorways and hallways and into their rooms. In less than ten minutes, the school settled quietly into the usual afternoon activities.

Mrs. Garcia listened for any unusual sounds from the students as they came back into the building. There were a couple of bangs of a door hitting a wall earlier in the recess period. That worried her a little. However, Gil hadn't reported any problems to her, and she was hearing only the regular noises as the kids returned from recess now. After a few minutes, she turned back to her magazine, pleased that the day was going so well. She felt proud of the youngsters for their good behavior.

Priscilla greeted her afternoon students and their parents at the entrance again. "Welcome!" she said to the new faces. "I'm Miss Melody's helper this afternoon." She was more relaxed now than she was with the morning group. It was probably her calm behavior that put the new kindergartners at ease.

Priscilla entered the classroom when all of her students were in the room. "I'm a Little Teacup" was playing on the CD player. The pupils had grouped around the kitchen play area, the building blocks, and the coloring table. To attract their attention, she uncovered a large glass bowl full of cookies and said, "I would like you all to come over and sit with me on the rug." When everyone was seated, she allowed each student to take a cookie. She said, "I am going to be helping Miss Melody by being your teacher this afternoon. For our first activity I am going to read you a story about cats. After that we will be making cat puppets."

"Goodie!" said one of the girls. After reading the short story, Priscilla held up a sample puppet she had made during the morning class and said, "This is Ethel. Here is how you can make your own puppet." She picked up a brown paper bag and showed them what to do. "The materials are already on your tables." In a short time they were at their work places, cutting and coloring.

The clock in Priscilla's kindergarten room read 1:20 P.M. She walked from table to table, answering questions and helping students. She had activities planned for the entire afternoon that she thought they would enjoy. These included finger painting; string art; building blocks; a sand table; and a play kitchen with plastic pots, dishes, and a play stove. She also scheduled another snack time. "I do believe I'm pretty good at this," she proudly said to herself.

As time passed and other activities were chosen, some children worked alone while others worked and played together. Most were talking to friends. They talked about different topics, like their pets, a birthday party, or a new bike. Priscilla realized that questions for her had stopped. They seemed to have forgotten she was even there. She strolled around the room, watching and listening.

One little girl was finishing up her cat puppet when she said to her friend, "My brother is sleeping in a tent in our backyard tonight. He asked me if I would sleep out there with him, but I said no. I hate bugs. Then he said to me, 'I'll give you five dollars if you stay and sleep in the tent with me.'"

"Wow!" said her friend. "Will you do it?"

She replied, "I said no. Then he told me he'd give me seven dollars and wouldn't be mean to me for a week. So I said okay."

"Will he be nice to you for a whole week?" asked the friend.

"I don't know, but I want the seven dollars!" She paused and said, "I hope it's worth it. I hate bugs."

Priscilla walked on and watched a little boy who was drawing a picture of a very strong man. As he added thicker muscles to an arm, the boy made explosion-like sounds. When he saw that Priscilla was watching, he held the drawing up for her to see. He said, "This is Superman. He's awesome!"

Priscilla said, "Wow! He looks so strong! Did you know there are comic books about him?"

The boy didn't answer; he began adding more muscles.

At the next table two other boys were also talking. "I like R movies, but my parents won't let me see them."

"Mine either," replied the other boy, "but they brought me to one, once. It was a movie they wanted to see real bad. There were a lot of swear words and fighting. I liked it." He covered his face with his hands as he giggled. His pal giggled too.

At the next table three girls were finger painting and chatting. "My mom went camping last month with my dad. I heard her say to our neighbor that she had toiletries with her. I guess it's a tree that is shaped like a toilet. That sounds really weird to me."

Her friend answered, "A toilet tree?"

Priscilla interrupted. "No no! *Toiletries* is a word for things in your bathroom, like toothpaste and soap. It's not about trees!"

"*Ohhh!*" said each of the girls at the same time. One of them touched her palm to her forehead. "I get it." Then her smile quickly disappeared. She said, "That's a yucky name for toothpaste and soap."

Priscilla walked on, smiling. "I didn't know listening to little kids was this much fun," she told herself.

Breaking Glass

With all the students back in their classrooms, Gil took a casual walk around the school again. He wanted to be sure the classes were settled down nicely after lunch. He started at the third-grade rooms.

Meanwhile, Kelly's fifth-grade class was busy talking about Thomas Jefferson. Duke was squirming in his seat, looking nervous, and thinking, "Why do I have to be the one to pull the fire alarm! Carl comes up with the big idea, and I get stuck doing it."

He took a hard look at Carl, who didn't notice. "*Humph!* No wonder he looks relaxed. I have to do all the dirty work!"

He glared at him again, and this time Carl returned his gaze, pointing to the classroom door. Duke angrily looked back, as if to say, "Don't rush me!" He quickly looked away. After a short pause, he took a deep breath. "Well, here goes nothing!" He got out of his seat and approached Kelly. "I need to go to the bathroom," he whispered.

"Okay," Kelly nodded and turned back to the class, continuing to discuss the third U.S. president. As he passed through the door, Duke looked back and saw that Carl and Wes were watching him.

He walked toward the fire alarm, which was down the hall, just outside the washroom. Right next to the alarm was the fire extinguisher. It was sitting on a shelf that was set into the wall, encased behind a small black door. He continued to gripe to himself about his situation. "I'm the one who's gonna get caught. Then I get suspended, and nothing happens to Carl and Wes. And they know I won't squeal on them."

Suddenly his mind switched back to what he was doing. He looked up and down the hallway thinking, "I have to be sure no one sees me." When he got to the fire alarm, he read the instructions through the glass. *To set off fire alarm break glass.* He'd seen these instructions a hundred times before. He slipped into the boys' washroom and looked at himself in the mirror. He knew he was stalling.

While Duke was trying to build up his nerve, Gil had left the kindergarten area and walked toward the fifth-grade rooms. When he got there, he decided to pay Kelly and his class a quick little visit.

Right after Gil entered Kelly's room, Duke pushed the boys' washroom door open and carefully stepped out. No one was in the hallway. He turned to face the fire alarm and read the instructions again: *To set off fire alarm break glass.* He quickly checked the hallway once more, then grabbed the handle. His heart began to beat harder as he held tight and yanked hard. The glass shattered and fell in small pieces to the floor. No one heard. "What's wrong?" he thought, "It's not going off!" He looked back at the alarm and saw the instructions inside the broken glass area. *Pull black handle down to sound alarm.* He took two more quick looks. Still no one! He grabbed the handle firmly.

Meanwhile, Gil said good-bye to Kelly and entered the hallway to continue checking on rooms. Immediately he spotted Duke down the hall, just standing there, facing the wall. Gil wondered, "What's he doing? He's gripping something on the wall. What is it? Oh shoot, it's the fire alarm!" Gil raced toward Duke. "Hey!" he yelled, never taking his eyes off Duke's hand.

Duke jumped when he heard Gil's voice. Gil was already half way up the hallway when Duke's eyes jerked back to the hand that he had wrapped around the handle. "Oh no!" he said. His face twisted in fear and confusion as he looked again at Gil.

"Duke, don't do it!" yelled Gil.

Duke didn't know whether to pull the handle or run, but his legs decided for him. He turned toward the fourth-grade entrance. "I'm getting out of here!" he yelled.

Dusty heard Gil's yells from the office. He gripped his pants at the waist and flew out into the hallway. When he turned the corner near the entrance door, he and Duke collided. Both boys fell to the floor in front of the door. Gil yelled to Dusty, "Hold him!"

Duke scrambled to his feet and tried to get to the door, but Dusty held on to Duke's shirt and yanked him back down. Duke tried to break free, but Dusty held tight, as his pants dropped to his knees. He held tight to Duke's shirt with one hand, and yanked his pants back up with the other. Out of nowhere Gil smashed down on top of both of them.

"Ooff!" The three boys grunted and ended up in a dis-combobulated pile. Arms and legs pointed everywhere. Gil and Dusty each had a hold on some part of Duke. He struggled a little more, and Gil said, "Duke . . . hold it . . . . What are you doing? Take it easy, will you?" Suddenly the struggle was over. All three boys lay in a heap on the floor, breathing heavily.

They sat for a moment, looking at each other. Some kids' heads poked out of their classrooms to see what was happening. Gil shouted, "It's okay, guys. We're just helping out a friend. Really, it's okay." He waved his arms, motioning them back into their rooms. One by one, the heads disappeared.

"Duke, were you going to pull that alarm?"

Duke lowered his head, still breathing heavily, and said, "Yeah!"

"Why?"

Duke shook his head, not sure of what to say. Gil looked around, realizing where they were. He said, "C'mon, let's get out of the hallway. We gotta talk."

All three boys got up and headed for the office. As they walked, Dusty continued to hold onto Duke's shirt with one hand. When they got to the principal's office, Gil closed the door and they all sat down.

"Why?" asked Gil.

Duke glared at Gil, then at Dusty. He was torn between being angry with them and feeling guilty about trying to pull the alarm.

Dusty repeated the question, "Why? What were you thinking?"

Duke explained everything that he, Wes, and Carl talked about.

Dusty said, "What! Geez! That would have ended it for us for sure! And it would have gotten us into even more trouble than we're already going to get into. Do you know it's illegal to make a false alarm?

"Yes, I know!" Duke snapped.

"What a really lousy idea! That would have sent us to juvenile jail or detention, whatever it's called," Gil complained. "We need to talk to Carl and Wes. Geez! Do you think they would be willing to talk with us?"

Duke shrugged his shoulders. "Wes would, but I'm not so sure about Carl."

"Dusty, would you go down to the classroom and see if you can get them to come here. I bet they're wondering why the alarm hasn't gone off yet. Tell them that Duke is with us."

Dusty sprang out of his chair and rushed out the door. When the three of them returned, Duke glared hard at Carl, but kept silent. Carl returned the scowl, then looked down at the floor.

They sat there for a moment before Wes spoke. "Do you know what it's like to be left out of something? Not very good! It's lousy!"

Carl broke in, "How do you think we feel?" he hissed. "And not just us!" He looked at Gil. "Big man in charge. Ha!" Carl continued, "We found out about your plan and that you kept it a secret from us. What were we supposed to do, be happy about it? It stinks. You did it again, Hodges! You take over without thinking of others; you only think about yourself."

Gil didn't want to have a huge fight when they were so close to finishing the day. He made himself stay calm. "Okay, I'm too bossy sometimes. It happens! I don't plan it that way. You're right, I didn't think about how you and the others would feel. I'm sorry, you guys."

"Well, leaving us out of it almost guaranteed that we'd do something to mess it up."

Gil said, "Is there anyone else you think might feel that way?"

Carl answered. "I hope so!" He hesitated, then said in a quieter tone, "No one that I know of."

"Good!" Gil said. "Look, I just thought of an idea of how to include you three in this plan. Would you promise to not ruin the takeover if we tell you a secret only some of us know about?"

Their faces lit up like a scoreboard, and all three of them replied at the same time, "Yeah!" They leaned a little forward as Gil told them about the intruder tied up in the basement.

"He's pretty sore from a whack on the head, and he's got a ton of tape wrapped around him. I know him from the neighborhood. I don't think he's such a dangerous guy, but right now he's pretty mad about what we've done to him. It would be a good idea if someone watched him for the rest of the day. He won't try to get out of the duct tape if he's being watched, but I don't know how long that tape can hold him. Do you guys think you could handle guarding him for the rest of the afternoon?"

"Sure!"

"But not all of you at the same time," warned Gil. "Only one at a time, in shifts, until school gets out. Then we tell Mrs. . . . . uh, then we call the police."

"We can do that!" said Wes.

"Okay, you guys figure out who watches him first. We'll take you to the basement to check him out."

Gil and Dusty stepped out of the office and waited as the three boys decided who would guard Hank first. A minute later they opened the office door. Carl announced, "I'm going first, Duke is going second, and Wes will be third."

They all walked down the hallway to the basement door. Gil instructed them, "Go halfway down the stairs. He's sitting on the floor at the other side of the room. He is duct-taped to a pipe. Take a look. Dusty and I will wait here for you up here. Come right back up."

Carl, Duke, and Wes cautiously walked through the doorway and started down the dark steps. They stayed very close to each other, with Carl a half step ahead of his buddies. They were careful not to make any noise. Halfway down, Carl stopped with a sudden jerk, and Duke and Wes slowly eased down next to him.

Hank knew someone was creeping down the stairs, but he couldn't see whom or how many. He fixed his eyes on the highest step he could see, halfway up. First one pair of sneakers appeared, then two more. It was quiet enough to hear them breathing.

The boys locked arms together, bent their knees, and lowered their heads to look at the man. He was sitting on the floor, staring back at them. His hair and clothes were mussed and dirty. Gray tape was wrapped around his wrists and ankles, and the tape around his chest bound him to a big pipe.

Hank stared at the curious faces looking down at him. He thought they looked like the Three Stooges in a ghost movie. If he weren't so uncomfortable, he would have laughed at them. Suddenly the boys turned and ran upstairs like scared mice. They slammed the door and rejoined Dusty and Gil.

"He's huge!" declared Wes.

Carl said, "He looks beat up. It must have taken a bunch of you to get him down."

Gil smiled. "Do you know Donny Mueller in fourth grade? He got him down and knocked him out. All we did was tie him up."

All three said together, "A fourth grader?"

"Yeah," said Dusty.

Gil got serious and gave instructions. "When it's your turn to go down there, just watch him. Don't talk to him because he may try to trick you. Don't get close to him. Sit on the stairway and stay there. If anything happens, run up here and slam the door. Stick this piece of wood under the door and kick it in tight, like this." Gil slid the wedge under the door and kicked it. He pulled on the doorknob to show that it was impossible to open. He wiggled the wedge out with his hand and placed it on the floor next to the door. "It will be right here."

They nodded.

"Okay, you start, Carl."

Carl looked at Duke and said, "Don't be late when it's your turn."

Duke and Wes went back to their room, and Gil and Dusty walked back to the office. "I think that will keep them happy till this is over, Dusty."

It was one thirty. An hour and a half of school to go.

Keep That Fan On

By two o'clock, Priscilla's students were spread out all over the room working at different activity centers. She walked around the room again, listening in and talking with some of her students. As she passed the sandbox table, she heard someone's stomach growling. She stood at the table for awhile. She saw that Eddie Stanky was holding his stomach. "Eddie, are you feeling okay?"

"My tummy hurts," he answered.

"Is it a bad tummy ache?" she asked.

"No. I told my mom at breakfast, and she said I should take it easy."

"Okay, Eddie, but tell me if it gets worse. I can take you to the nurse's office if you start to feel worse. Okay?"

"Okay!" As she spoke, Eddie's hands were busy making small roads in the sand for his little cars. She strolled away but decided to keep an eye on him.

As she got involved with other students, she noticed the worried expression on Eddie's face. Some of the girls were setting the play table in the kitchen area when Eddie walked past them and into the little washroom in their classroom. Priscilla spotted him as he closed the washroom door. He had a pained look on his face.

"Uh oh!" she thought. "I hope he doesn't throw up. That would be a total gross-out."

She got worried when Eddie didn't come out of the washroom after five minutes, so she decided to check on him. She knocked on the door. "Eddie?"

He didn't answer. She heard him through the door. He was crying.

"Eddie, are you all right?" She thought, "I'm sure he's thrown up. Oh gosh, I hope I can get through this."

Eddie's crying became louder, so Priscilla knocked lightly again. She slowly cracked the door open and peeked in. The room had a very strong odor. She saw Eddie sitting on the toilet inside the stall next to the white sink. His pants were down around his ankles. He looked up at her through his tears. He had diarrhea and had made a mess all over his pants and legs. He didn't know what to do, so he just sat there sniffling.

Priscilla stepped in and pulled the bathroom door closed, looking away from Eddie. She switched on the ceiling fan and began to think. "What do I do now? What would Miss Melody do? Oh, this smell is making me gag."

There was a knock at the door. "Is Eddie in there?" asked Eddie's pal.

Priscilla raised her voice. "Yes, Eddie's here. It's okay, Tommy. We'll be out soon."

With her back to her student, she said, "Okay, Eddie, I'm going to leave for a minute. You stay here. It'll be okay. Don't worry." She opened and closed the door quickly and hurried to the classroom door. She looked in the hallway for someone to help her while she was thinking about what to do. She saw Sarah walking back to her own classroom. She had just dropped her students off at art class.

Priscilla sounded desperate. "Sarah!" she called and hurried toward her. Sarah stopped and waited as Priscilla blurted out, "Eddie Stanky just pooped all over himself in the bathroom!"

"What?"

"It's so gross! It smells like a barn in there. He's crying, and I don't know what to do, Sarah. He needs help."

Sarah said, "Why don't you go in there and clean him up?"

"What? I can't do that!" said Priscilla.

"You can't just leave him in there. How about helping him wash himself? He can do that."

"Yes!" said Priscilla. "Then I wouldn't have to touch him."

Sarah said, "I'll see if I can find a pair of pants in the lost-and-found box."

"Okay thanks, Sarah!" she answered. As she turned to leave, she said, "Wish me luck!" Priscilla hurried back to her room, muttering to herself, "Clean him up! I'm only ten years old. I'm too young to be doing this."

When she entered the classroom, she forced a smile as she looked around the room. The students were still playing nicely, but Tommy's eyes followed her as she walked by.

Priscilla knocked lightly on the washroom door and slipped back in. She held her nose. Eddie looked glad that she was back. He wasn't crying anymore. Priscilla went right to work. She ran warm water in the sink and pulled paper towels out of the holder as fast as she could. She kept her eyes off Eddie, thinking he would be embarrassed. She said, "Kick off those pants, Eddie; you can't wear them anymore. Take off your shoes and socks too. Let's get you cleaned up."

"Okay," he said.

Soon, Eddie was naked from the waist down. "Okay, Priscilla," he said. He hugged himself like he was chilled.

Priscilla grabbed a handful of paper towels, then soaked them in warm water. She kept herself facing away from the little boy. She reached back and handed the towels to Eddie, saying. "Wash yourself really well with these towels, and then throw them in this trash basket. Start at your waist and work your way down. I'll keep giving you fresh ones until you are clean."

Eddie did as he was told. He worked slowly at first, but soon he was wiping himself quickly with the dripping towels. He looked at Priscilla every few seconds. Priscilla never peeked. Eddie's lower body was soaked. The warm water felt good at first, and then it cooled and didn't feel as good. When he finished washing his legs, he said in a weak voice, "I'm clean."

Priscilla handed him a pile of dry paper towels. "Now dry yourself." She cracked the door open to check on her students. They had to be wondering what was wrong, but only Tommy was watching the washroom door. She smiled at him and gave him the thumbs-up sign.

Eddie said, "I'm dry, but I don't have any pants to wear."

"Don't worry about that. Stay here, and keep that fan on. I'm going to find you a clean pair of pants." She walked over to Tommy, who asked, "What's wrong with Eddie?"

"He had an upset stomach, but he's okay now. He's coming out soon."

Just then Sarah rushed to Priscilla's classroom door with a pair of brown pants and a plastic trash bag. She said, "Whitey got the bag for me." She handed them to Priscilla. "How is he?"

"He's better, Sarah. You saved my life! Eddie's too! He was a total mess." She took the pants and bag and said, "Thanks!"

Sarah smiled. "You're welcome. See you later." She walked back to her room.

Priscilla knocked on the bathroom door again and handed Eddie the pants and plastic bag. She spoke through the door opening. "Put these pants on, Eddie, and put your other pants and underpants in the plastic bag, and close it. Are your shoes and socks clean?"

"My shoes are clean, but my socks are yucky."

"Put your socks in the bag too. Just wear shoes. How do you feel?"

"My tummyache is gone. I feel okay now," he answered.

"Do you want to go back and play with Tommy, or do you want to go to the nurse's office?"

"I want to play with Tommy."

"Good! Stuff the plastic bag in the wastebasket, wash your hands, and come out when you're ready."

✳ ✳ ✳

A little later, Sarah stopped back in Priscilla's room to see how things were going. Priscilla had just finished reading the class a story about a boy named Alexander, who was having a very bad day. Priscilla was watching some boys drawing army tanks when Sarah walked up beside her.

"Which one is Eddie?" she whispered.

Priscilla tipped her head slightly toward a little boy in a pair of slightly oversized, brown pants. He was pushing a toy truck around on the floor with a friend. The two girls smiled at each other. Sarah whispered, "I wonder how often a kindergarten teacher has that happen to her?"

Priscilla said, "I hope not ever."

Sarah left to pick up her students from art class. Priscilla began another tour of the room. The fan in the washroom remained on for the rest of the afternoon.

Water and Straw

Kelly's students were well into their afternoon activities. They were sitting on the floor listening to Kelly read from a novel called *Summer of the Monkeys*. It was Mrs. Garcia's favorite children's book. She read for twenty minutes. Science was the next subject. It had already been arranged by Mrs. Garcia that three of her students were to give demonstrations that day.

"Kristen, are you ready to do your presentation?" asked Kelly. Kristen Hunt nodded and strode to the front of the room. Before she began to speak, Kelly reminded Kristen about the usual classroom procedure. "Don't forget to ask for questions when you're finished."

Kristen nodded that she understood and immediately showed everyone a large plastic straw that she had gotten from a fast-food restaurant. In her other hand she held up a pair of scissors. She announced, "Um, I am going to change this straw, um, into a horn, and play a musical scale. It shows, uh, how the length of a musical instrument, uh, makes a higher or lower sound."

Someone yelled, "It's a fake straw, right?"

"Uh-uh!" Kristen shook her head no. "Look!" She held the straw out between her thumb and index finger and turned it at different angles so the class could see.

She put it to her mouth and blew through it. Nothing but swishing air flowed from the other end. "First, uh, I have to cut it a certain way. Watch."

Kristen snipped twice at one end of the straw with the scissors, shaping it like an arrowhead. She squeezed the pointed end together with her fingers and said, "I'm going to bite down on this tip really hard. After pressing it together, the end will begin to flatten. Then I'm going to put it in my mouth and blow really hard. If it, uh, works, the part that I cut will vibrate, and that will be my, uh, first musical note. It should sound like a buzzer."

The class watched as she put the pointed end in her mouth and flattened the tip with her front teeth. A few of the students didn't believe it would work. "It's good to get spit on it too, because that kind of, uh, softens it." She bit a little while longer and then announced, "Here goes."

She put the flattened end in her mouth and blew so hard they thought her eyes were going to pop out. Nothing but air came out of the end of the straw. "Wait!" she requested. She drowned the tip in more spit and bit again. Then she drew a huge breath and blew hard.

"*Blllzzzzzzt!*" It was a rough, raspy sound, loud enough to be heard a hundred feet away.

Someone said, "Wow!"

"Cool!"

"Do it again!"

Kristen blew again.

"*Blllzzzzzzzzzzzzzzt!*" All the faces in the room were beaming.

Kelly, acting like a teacher, said, "Let's hear you make different notes."

"Okay," said Kristen. She held up the scissors and said, "I'm going to cut the straw to make it shorter. I'll shorten it seven times. I'll do *doe–re–mi* up to *doe* again."

She placed the straw up to her mouth and held the opened scissors near the far end of the straw. She took another deep breath and blew out that raspy sound again. As she took the next breath, she cut off about an inch of straw and blew again. This note was higher. After another breath and another inch cut off, an even higher note sounded. When she made the last cut, only about two inches of straw remained. She took one final breath and raised her arm, like a singer at the end of a song, and blew as hard as her lungs and cheeks could push. *"Zeeeeeeeeeeeet!"* came the final note, right on the high *doe* note.

"Yay!" cheered the students, including Kelly. Kristen was tired and smiling. When the others quieted down, she asked, "Are there any questions?"

One of her friends said, "Can you play Happy Birthday?"

Another person yelled, "That was cool, Kristen. I never knew a straw could make a noise like that." There were no other questions. Kristen giggled and sat down, relieved and proud that her demonstration was a success.

Kelly wasted no time. "Daryl, are you ready for your presentation?" She spoke in her teacher's voice.

"Yes," was his loud response, "except I have to fill my bucket with water first." He slid from his seat and filled his plastic one-gallon bucket from the classroom sink. He leaned to one side as he carried it. Kelly saw that the water was almost to the top edge. He stood at the front of the classroom and placed the bucket very carefully by his feet.

Kelly said to a student, "Jonathan, would you please close the door." He did. Daryl began his almost completely memorized presentation. "Centripetal force is what is necessary to keep an object moving in a circular path. An example would be a stone that is tied to a string and is swung around in a circle. Centripetal force is exerted on the stone." Daryl drew large circles in the air with his arm to illustrate.

"Now I will use this bucket of water to show centripetal force. I will swing the bucket up and down in a circle over my head. The centripetal force will prevent the water from falling out of the bucket."

The class began sitting up like they were more interested. They were hoping water would soon be all over the front of the classroom, and if they were lucky, on top of Daryl's head. Kelly looked nervous. "Have you done this experiment before, Daryl?"

He smiled, knowing why Kelly asked. "Sure," he bragged, "I've done this a dozen times."

"And the water stayed in the bucket?" asked Kelly.

"Every drop," Daryl boasted.

Kelly wrinkled her brow, looked at the class and said, "Okay, let's see *cen-tep-i-tral force,* or whatever it's called." Kelly reminded Daryl about Mrs. Garcia's rule.

Daryl picked up the bucket and began swinging back and forth, each swing going higher than the one before. The students wiggled themselves higher in their seats, hoping. Daryl's eyes became fixed on an empty space across the room as the bucket arched higher and higher. Suddenly he continued the arc into a complete and rapid circle over his head. As the bucket passed upside down the water remained in the bucket. Daryl flashed a smile at the class as his arms swung in big circles. He looked like a high-speed windmill.

"Whoa!" they exclaimed. "How'd he do that?" Their eyes stayed on the bucket during each revolution. Kelly looked surprised.

After a while, Daryl brought the bucket to a stop on the upswing, keeping the top of the bucket facing the ceiling. A few drops spilled out.

"That was neat!" said some kids. Others clapped. Daryl placed the bucket on the floor and took a bow. Everyone clapped.

Someone yelled, "Aw, anybody could do that!"

"Can I try?" asked another student. Immediately fourteen hands shot up. Daryl looked at Kelly.

Kelly shrugged her shoulders. "I guess so. What do you think, Daryl?"

"Sure!" Daryl knew it wasn't that easy, and thought it would be fun to see someone make a mess. Every hand was up now. He picked his friend Artie Nilson, who rushed out of his seat and ran to the front of the room.

Daryl filled the bucket to the top again. He said to his pal, "Swing it back and forth a few times first, and then when you swing over the top, go fast and hard. Keep going fast. If you slow down, you'll spill it." Daryl stepped off to the side. Students in the front row moved back a few seats.

Artie grabbed the plastic handle and picked up the bucket. He began swinging the bucket back and forth. "Swing harder," instructed Daryl. Artie soon had the bucket swinging up to shoulder height.

"C'mon, Artie! Over the top," yelled one of his friends. Finally, he quickened his arm movement and over it went. It worked! He swung harder and faster and not a drop spilled. The students cheered again. Artie beamed as his arm spun.

Then he made a mistake. He lost his concentration and slowed his arm when the bucket was directly over-head. The water splashed down onto him, soaking his head and shirt. The class exploded in laughter, pointing and clapping as Artie choked. He wiped his face and hair as he put the bucket down. Kelly and Daryl were laughing so hard they couldn't talk. Artie whipped both arms down, trying to shake off the water.

Kelly calmed herself. "Artie, I hope you have an extra shirt in your locker, because you are soaked." That brought more laughter and clapping.

Daryl rushed up to Artie and turned to the class. He yelled, "Are there any questions?"

More laughter. One of his classmates yelled out, "Does Artie know how to swim?" Artie left the room to get a dry shirt.

Another yelled, "Can I try it?"

Kelly cut in quickly, "Wait, wait, wait! We'd better get on with the next experiment. Thank you, Daryl, for a very interesting demonstration. I don't think we will forget this one for a very long time." Daryl bowed again toward Kelly and received his final ovation from the class. He and some friends wiped up the puddles from the tile floor with paper towels.

The Bowl

H ank had been sitting on the basement floor for over two hours. His back hurt, and almost every muscle was sore. He tried shifting positions, but that gave him almost no relief. "At least my head is clear, and I don't feel sick to my stomach anymore. How could I let that little pip-squeak get the best of me?"

His thoughts turned to Carl, the first student that came down to guard him. "I'm glad that weirdo kid is gone. He gawked at me for half an hour. That boy looked different . . . angry and mean. I would never get anywhere talking to him."

"The second boy on the stairs was more like a normal ten-year-old," Hank thought. He tried to get him to talk by asking what grade he was in.

"Fifth," Duke answered. He looked away though because he knew he shouldn't be answering questions.

"Do you like this school?"

"Yeah!"

"I used to go here, ya know." Duke looked at Hank and then looked away.

"That last room in the hallway was my fifth-grade room. I had Mrs. Lowenstein."

Duke offered, "She retired when I was in third grade."

"Yeah?" replied Hank. "I liked her. She was okay."

Suddenly the door opened at the top of the stairs. Hank was disappointed that the next kid was coming; he thought maybe he could have tricked Duke somehow and made an escape.

Duke scampered up the steps. At the top of the stairs the two boys whispered too low for Hank to hear. Then it got quiet. Wes, the third boy to guard the man, closed the hallway door and slowly came down the steps. He sat on the same step where Duke had been and put his elbows on his knees and his hands under his chin. He took a quick glance at Hank but looked away when he saw Hank looking back at him.

Wes thought, "He looks different now, dirtier than before." Then Wes shifted into a new sitting position, glancing at the corners of the basement, the floor, his feet, and then the ceiling.

Hank thought, "This one is nervous. If I'm going to get out of here, I'd better work this kid fast. I've got less than thirty minutes."

He said aloud, "Hi. My name's Hank."

Wes crossed his arms over his chest. He inspected cobwebs hanging from the ceiling, dusty old books on a table, a flattened basketball. He was working hard to avoid eye contact.

"What's your name?"

Wes ignored him.

"It's okay, kid. I'm all tied up here. You can tell me your name, can't you?"

Wes held his arms tighter around his chest, but Hank kept trying to get him to talk. He explained, "I can't break through this tape. I just asked your name. That's not a crime."

Wes looked up and whispered, "Wes."

"What?" prodded Hank. "I didn't hear you. What is it?"

He answered louder now, "Wes!"

Hank smiled. "Wes! Good! I have a cousin named Wes. His whole name is Wesley. He's a good guy. Lives over in Maplewood." After a short pause, he added, "I guess you're in fifth grade too, huh?"

Wes answered reluctantly, "Yeah."

"Hey, Wes. I only saw kids upstairs. Where are the teachers?"

No answer.

"Okay, I don't blame you. I'd be careful, too, if I were you." Hank never took his eyes off the boy. He studied him, searching a way to win his trust. "I was just wondering why no teachers came into the bathroom when I was hurt."

Minutes went by. Hank was getting impatient as Wes kept ignoring him. "What time have you got, Wes?"

Wes waited, then looked at his watch, then waited a while longer. Finally, he muttered, "2:36."

"Thanks, Wes."

More minutes crawled by. Both of them shifted their sitting positions. Hank's face twisted in pain as he moved. Finally he broke the long silence. "I don't think I can make it." Wes shot him a look. "I mean, I've been here all afternoon. I don't think I can wait before messing my pants. I have to go really bad."

Wes sat still. "He's trying to trick me," he thought.

"I'm not kidding. I'm going to wet my pants. I haven't gone since after breakfast."

Wes answered firmly, "Then you're going to just have to wet yourself. I am not moving from this spot."

"Oh, Wes," moaned Hank. "Please don't make me mess myself."

"I am not going to untie you. Sorry." He sounded firm.

Hank let a minute go by, then he began to moan. "You don't have to untie me. Grab that bowl over there. I'll use that."

"Sick!" Wes squealed. "That's disgusting!"

"I know." Hank wailed, "but I'm desperate! I don't want to be all wet and cold, and I won't have any other clothes to wear when I leave here."

Wes looked at his watch. 2:41! Hank figured that Wes was hoping to wait it out until the bell rang, when someone else would come down to handle the situation. Hank couldn't let that happen.

Hank pleaded, "I can't hold it any longer. Please! I'm begging! You don't have to untie me, just bring that bowl over here. You don't have to watch." He was crying now. "You can sit at the top of the stairs while I go. Just look the other way. Please! I'm begging you. Don't make me wet my pants."

Wes looked at him and then at the bowl with paint-color stains. He stood up, walked quickly to the bowl, and picked it up with two fingers. It was covered with dust. He blew hard into it, and a cloud of dust flew up into his face. "Phew!" He coughed once and wiped his face with his arm. He turned and walked toward Hank. He decided to place the bowl on the floor just outside of Hank's reach. Then he was going to sit on the highest step on the stairway, as Hank suggested. As he approached the prisoner, he said, "I don't plan on emptying this for you. You'll just have to keep it near you until later."

Hank croaked, "Yes, yes. That's okay. That's a lot better than sitting in wet pants. Thank you. Thank you!" His eyes stayed fixed on the bowl. Wes bent down and placed the bowl in a safe spot. At exactly the right moment, Hank jerked out his tied hands and caught Wes's wrist in a vise grip.

"*Agh!*" yelled Wes.

Hank pulled the boy to the floor. Wes was now Hank's prisoner. He was lying with his back on Hank's lap and his lower half was on the floor. The only sounds in the basement were the bowl rolling away and Wes's quick breathing.

"No!" Wes yelped. He pulled, twisted, and kicked as hard as he could, but Hank's powerful hands held him. Hank then wrapped his hands around Wes's neck. Wes could smell the man's breath. His eyes began to fill with tears. "Oh no! Please!"

Hank's grasp was firm but not painful. He put his mouth next to Wes's ear. He whispered in a friendly tone,

"I'm sorry I had to trick you, Wes. I won't hurt you, but I need your help getting me out of this tape."

Wes was panting, but he stopped struggling. He was lying completely on top of the man and helplessly looking up at the ceiling.

"Please don't hurt me!" he pleaded.

"Of course not, Wes. There is no need for me to hurt you. We've become good friends in this short time. You tried to help me, remember? Oh yes, you and I are friends. I think you are a great guy. Just relax now. Take a few breaths."

The boy closed his eyes and relaxed the tense muscles in his arms and legs. "Good! Good!" coaxed Hank. "You're feeling better already. That's good."

Wes shifted his eyes from side to side, looking for a stick or anything that might make a good weapon. The plastic bowl was useless, and the broom leaning against the wall was too far away.

"Now, here's what I want you to do. I'm going to turn you around to face me. I want you to find the end of the tape that is wrapped around my wrists. I want you to peel the end of the tape back and pull it loose. That's all. Once my hands are free, I'll let you go. I will undo the tape around my waist and ankles myself. That's it! Now, we haven't much time. I'd like to leave this school before all the kids go home."

He loosened his grip around the boy's neck. "Now, slowly turn around and face me. Don't make any sudden movements; just turn slowly until you can see the tape around my wrists. Go ahead."

Wes didn't move. He thought that if he freed the man's hands, he would be hurt anyway. Hank's grip tightened again, and his voice turned harsh. "Wes! I'm asking you nicely. I'm not in a good position right now, and you are the only one who can help me. Turn toward me right now." Hank applied more pressure on the boy's neck and turned it slightly to the right.

"Ahh!" squeaked Wes. "That hurts!"

"Turn!' barked Hank. "Please!"

Wes pushed and shifted his body onto his right side. When he was almost completely turned around, the two prisoners looked at each other. One face was worried; the other one was scared. With a sudden movement, Hank shifted his grip from Wes's neck to his arm and held him away from his body. He wanted to allow the boy a view of his wrapped wrists. He snapped, "Look at the tape. Find the end and peel it back. Do it fast!"

Wes began digging at the end of the tape with his fingernails. He loosened it enough to grab hold of the tape with his fingers. He made short rips at first, but then he was able to pull off larger lengths of tape.

"Good!' said Hank. "Keep going!" He kept his eyes on the tape as more and more of it was removed. Wes pulled faster, working circles around Hank's wrists. The amount of loose tape got longer and longer.

"Agh!" screeched Hank. Removing the tape ripped

hair off Hank's wrists, but suddenly his hands were not bound together anymore. He rubbed one of his wrists against his chest, as if to scratch an itch. He held tightly onto Wes's arm with his other hand. Wes threw the loosened tape down onto Hank and shifted to get up on his feet. His job was done. He was ready to go.

"Wait!" snapped Hank, who was still holding onto Wes.

"You promised!" whined Wes.

"Sorry, kid. You'll tell everyone about me, and I'll never get out of here. Help me get the tape off my ankles, and I'll leave you here." Hank said it like it was a logical plan, but he put his free hand around Wes's neck again, reminding him who was in charge.

"That's not fair!" Wes complained. He tried to get up, but Hank applied more pressure. Wes stopped resisting.

"I know it's not fair, but that's the way it is." Hank pushed him down toward his ankles and spat out his command, "Start! Now!"

Wes peeled away the tape from Hank's ankles. A tear dropped onto Hank's jeans. Hank raised his feet off the floor as Wes ripped off each strip of tape. Soon, Hank's legs were free. "Good, Wes. Now get the tape off my chest, please."

Wes loosened the end of the tape, and it came off easily as he reached around the pipe and pulled off the tape. In a minute the tape was all removed. Hank was free after spending over two hours on the cold basement floor. Wes searched Hank's eyes for a clue about what was going to happen to him. Hank noted his fear.

"Here's what happens." Hank's voice was different now. He spoke like a sergeant giving orders to one of his men. "I have to leave you down here. I'm going up those stairs and getting out of here. I haven't hurt you. Remember that. You can unwrap the tape yourself, but by then I'll be gone. I hope you and I are still friends."

Wes didn't answer. He was relieved to hear he was going to be left alone, but he was still scared. He wanted to get away from this man. Hank suddenly stood up with the used tape in his hand. He held Wes's arm next to the pipe and wrapped it so many times that the arm disappeared from view. "Ow! That hurts. It's tight."

"That's okay, Wes, it won't hurt for long. You can peel this off in no time with your free hand. So long, kid," Hank smiled. "It's been a pleasure getting to know you."

Wes looked away from Hank. His taped arm was already beginning to feel like pins and needles. Hank hurried up the stairs, taking two steps at a time. Wes watched him disappear and began tearing off the tape. It was easier to do this time.

Hank cracked open the door and squinted at the brightness. He rushed to his right and looked down the fourth-grade hallway. All he saw were lockers and a shiny floor. "Not a soul in sight," he thought. "Good! It's about time I caught a break." He ran toward the fourth-grade exit. Freedom at last!

White Chemical Particles

At 2:50 P.M., Gil, Leo, and Dusty sat in the school office, bursting with energy, ready to celebrate. It was the best trick that students ever played, at any school, in the whole world!

Leo bounced up and down on his tiptoes. "Come on, clock. Move!"

"Right," added Dusty. "I wish we knew how to ring the bell. A couple of minutes early wouldn't hurt."

"It'll come," Gil said. "We can wait another ten minutes."

Leo said, "I can't just sit here. It's killing me. Let's go check up on Wes."

Dusty said, "Okay."

Gil said, "You two go. I'll stay here."

As Leo and Dusty headed for the basement, Hank was hurrying down the hallway and almost at the exit door. He saw the two boys coming around the corner and stopped about ten feet in front of them. Leo and Dusty also stopped short and grabbed onto each other. "Oh!" exclaimed Dusty.

Hank showed a harsh smile. "Hello, boys!" he said in a friendly tone.

Leo's voice was shaky. "Where's Wes?"

The man jerked a thumb over this shoulder. "He's still in the basement."

"Did you hurt him?" asked Dusty.

Hank shook his head. "Oh no, he's okay, but he's unraveling a mile of tape." He turned serious. "I'm leaving now. You boys can go down and check on your pal. Go ahead." He stepped aside, waving his arm for them to pass.

Dusty did his best to sound tough. "You can't leave, Mister. It'll spoil everything."

Hank squinted like he was confused, and asked, "Spoil what? Wait! I don't care what's going on in this school. I just need to get out of here. Right now!" He looked toward the fourth-grade exit.

Leo and Dusty glanced at each other. They were both thinking the same thing. They stood up straight and put their hands on their hips, akimbo style. Their bodies were saying, "Yeah? Well, you are not getting past us!"

"What! I have to deal with you guys too?" Hank complained. He began to walk toward the two boys. Leo backed up a few steps and shifted to his right, blocking Hank's path to the door. Hank focused on Leo and the door. Dusty sidestepped off to the left, where he spotted the fire extinguisher on the wall. Hank growled at Leo, "Outta my way, you little twerp." Leo spotted Dusty quietly opening the fire extinguisher cabinet and grabbing the tank.

"Wait!" Leo said to Hank, trying to keep his attention focused on him. He held up his hand like a policeman. "Promise me that you didn't hurt my friend Wes."

"What are you talking about?" Hank said. "Get outta my way." He made a move toward Leo. Dusty let go of his pants quickly and jerked the plastic pin out of its slot near the handle of the fire extinguisher. He approached Hank from behind, pointing the nozzle toward the man's head. Hank said to Leo, "Look, pal, I never hurt a kid before, but I will if you try to stop me."

Dusty said, "Ahem!" Hank turned to look. With his pants down around his ankles, Dusty squeezed the handle and a loud sound whooshed out of the extinguisher as white chemicals shot all over Hank's head, face, and shoulders.

"*Agh!*" he hollered. His hands went to his face while Dusty kept firing. His entire head and shoulders were covered in white goop. While Hank staggered, Leo dove and wrapped his arms around the intruder's knees and pushed him to the floor. Dusty put the fire extinguisher down and pulled up his pants. Hank rolled on the floor, moving his legs back and forth as he tried to clear his eyes. He wailed, "I'm blind! I can't see!" Dusty picked up the fire extinguisher again. When Hank tried to get up, Dusty leaned over him and drove the bottom of the fire extinguisher into his stomach. "*Oowwfff!*" uttered the blinded man as he lay on the floor. Leo grabbed hold of Hank's legs.

At the far end of the hallway the basement door blew open, and Wes burst out. He spotted Hank lying on the floor at the far end of the hall. Wes charged forward with new courage. "Let me at him!" he yelled. He dove onto

Hank's chest. Dusty put the tank down to get his pants back up again. Hank wiped his face with one hand and tried to push Wes off with the other.

Leo said, "What do we do now?"

Dusty barked at Wes, "Get the duct tape. It's on the front desk in the office. Fast!"

Wes pushed off Hank and ran, full speed, toward the office. Leo hung tight to the helpless man's legs. He said to Dusty, "Drown him with that stuff if he tries to stand up."

Gil came running back with Wes. Gil looked down at Hank and gasped, "Oh no, not again!" He immediately wrapped Hank's feet while Hank was still clearing his eyes. They dragged him into the washroom again and then taped his hands and feet onto the metal legs of a stall. Gil said, "Sorry about this, Hank, but we've got to finish what we started."

Hank spit out particles of white chemicals onto the floor. He looked up at Dusty through blinking eyes and said, "All right, all right! Man, you kids are vicious! Gil, what's going on with you guys? I've never seen school kids this nasty."

"Hank, we're about to make history." Helpless, Hank looked under the stall and saw the bottom of the white toilet. "Oh no!" he said. "In the bathroom again?"

Gil looked at his watch and then said to his buddies, "School ends in three minutes. Let's get back into the office." Dusty turned to Wes and asked, "You know how to use this thing?" He pointed to the extinguisher.

"Sure, just squeeze that handle."

"That's right. Can you stay here with this guy until school empties out?"

"I sure can!" exclaimed Wes.

"Use it on him again if he tries to leave. We have to keep him here until all the kids are gone."

"Sure." Wes looked down at the man with a smile. "Don't worry! Hank won't go anywhere. He and I are friends."

* * *

During the fight with the intruder, the Central School students were preparing to go home. Priscilla's class was lining up with their new puppets and other artwork in their hands. "You were very good students this afternoon," she said. "Good-bye, and be sure to show your family your puppets." She opened the door, and the little kids burst into the hallway and rushed out to join their waiting parents or older siblings.

Sarah told her second-grade students that she really liked being their teacher and that she had had a good time with them. She stood at the classroom door and flashed good-bye smiles as they filed into the hallway. She held out her hand and they high-fived her as they passed. Some of the students even hugged her, and she hugged them back. She added, "Have a great day! See you on Monday!"

"Are we going to do this again next week?" asked a student.

"Are you kidding?" answered Sarah. "I really don't think so." She laughed when she saw the disappointed look on the child's face. She said, "I'll see you at lunch recess."

The girl who gave the tissue to her stepped up to Sarah and asked, "Will you get in trouble for this?"

Sarah's smile faded. "I don't know, Jennie."

The girl answered, "I hope not!" and rushed out of the room to join her friends. "Bye!" she waved.

Bobby said good-bye to all his third graders but made a special effort to pat Alvin on the back. "Any problems with that arm, Alvin?"

"Naw, it feels fine, Bobby."

"Good! Back to normal next week."

"See you, Bobby."

Kelly's class had put away all their books, pens, and pencils. Her students were standing at their desks, which is what they did at the end of every school day. Kelly said, "Well, it sure has been fun, you guys! Thanks for not giving me a hard time. Now I know what it feels like to be a teacher when students do dangerous science experiments. Artie, are you dry yet?" Everyone laughed.

"No," he said with a big smile.

Kelly finished by saying, "Well, back to normal on Monday . . . at least I hope so. Who knows what's going to happen to us now! Okay, see you." She waved her hand toward the door and the fifth graders filed out.

No Homework

Wes sat on the washroom floor close to Hank, with his hand on the handle of the fire extinguisher. They were quiet, waiting for the dismissal bell to ring. Gil, Dusty, and Leo were back in the office. The clock read 2:59 P.M. Their eyes were fixed on the red second hand of the clock as it glided around the numbers. Only one more minute to go before "Mission Accomplished."

Gil began thinking about what to do with Hank. His neighbor was probably in more trouble than he was. He didn't want to make life worse for him. Should he let him go or turn him in? He chose to wait until the school was empty before he made a decision.

The bell rang. Students spilled out of their rooms, locker doors opened, and jackets were yanked off hooks. The conversations were lively. An eight-year-old student shouted to her friend, "We finished Math early so we took turns telling jokes. It was so much fun."

A fourth grader asked, "What was all that laughing in Mrs. Garcia's room?"

"I don't know. We heard it too."

"Whatever it was, they sure laughed hard."

Another girl told her friends, "We played Heads-Up–Seven-Up for the last hour."

"My mom will never believe me when I tell her," laughed one second grader. "She'll think I'm making it up."

Another girl shouted, "Let's do this again, soon!"

One of Bobby's third graders boasted, "We didn't get any homework. Yay!"

A friend answered, "We didn't either." Then he realized, "Hey! I bet no one got homework tonight. Ha! First time in history that the whole school got zero homework. Yippee!"

Sadie said good-bye to her fourth-grade students as they left the room. When Donny was leaving, she spoke softly to him. "What a day, huh, Donny? Sorry about that comma lesson." Donny's answer was a smile; then he just rushed off.

The students enjoyed the sunny October air. Parents and neighbors were outside, standing around, waiting to take the children home. Some were sitting in their cars waiting. Bike racks were busy beehives as kids mounted their bikes and pedaled away. The students flowed onto different sidewalks like a river forking into different directions. Some wore backpacks; many were empty-handed. Everyone was talking about the exciting day they had at school.

There were more comments:

"Do you think Mr. Wilkins will be mad when he finds out? We'll tell him how hard we worked."

"I didn't believe her when Sadie told us she was the teacher."

"I never thought it would last the whole day. I didn't think we'd finish out the morning."

"I bet Gil and those guys will get into a lot of trouble for this. Mr. Alston is going to blow his stack."

"Yeah! Dancing eyebrows on Monday."

"Do you think we'll ever get another day like this again?"

"Are you kidding? Stoney will set up someone to check the school every day, including weekends."

Eventually the cars all drove off, the bike racks were deserted, and the sidewalks were bare. It looked like any other quiet day in the neighborhood. Anyone driving by would never suspect that the school they were passing would be in the newspapers, on the radio, and on television in just a few hours.

Not So Fast

After all the students had left the school, and the fifth-grade "teachers" had also left their rooms, Kelly and Sadie raised their fists in the air as they walked toward the office. Kelly said, "We did it! I can't believe it!" They came together with a two-handed high five and hugged each other.

"Let's go to the office," said Sadie.

"Okay! Sadie, did you happen to hear a strange buzzing noise coming from my room?" asked Kelly.

"Yes, I did. It sounded like a party horn. What was it?"

"It was a straw! Just a regular drinking straw. Kristen Hunt made a horn out of a straw."

Sadie said, "I heard a lot of laughing after that. What was that?"

"Oh," said Kelly. "Artie Nilson decided he'd like to try Daryl Wick's water experiment, and he ended up dumping a pail of water over his head. We all cracked up, and Artie was totally soaked. He laughed too. How about you, Sadie? How did your afternoon go?"

"It was a lot easier than I thought after what happened with Donny Mueller in the morning! Donny came in from lunch like a totally different person. He made us promise not to tell anyone, then told us a crazy story about a man sneaking into our school. I don't think anyone believed him. By the way, Mrs. Garcia is around somewhere. Let's check with Gil in the office and see what's happening now.

They met Sarah and Priscilla outside the office door. "Woo! Woo! What a great day!" exclaimed Priscilla.

"Ooooh yeah!" answered Sadie and Kelly. "Fifth-grade rules!" They high-fived each other and then paraded into the school office. Bobby and Whitey were already there. They all raised their arms up over their heads like they'd just won the Super Bowl. "We did it!" Kelly shouted. "We did it!"

Bobby began chanting, "Tee-chers! Tee-chers!" Everyone joined in. "Tee-chers! Tee-chers! Tee-chers!" The other "teachers" heard the chant and hurried into the office.

"Hey, this is like a victory party!" said Phil. "We are the only students in the world who have ever taken over a school!" Everyone cheered again.

Whitey yelled, "Let's go into the teachers' lounge for one last time."

In the lounge they traded stories. Leo told a couple of friends how he took care of Alvin's arm. "I thought it was broken, but first I treated him for shock."

Priscilla told some friends about Eddie Stanky and how Sarah saved her during a difficult situation. "I saw Sarah in the hallway and said, 'What do I do?' and she told me to clean him up. Then she got another pair of pants for him."

Sarah blushed when the others looked at her. "Nice going, Sarah!" shouted a classmate.

Bobby put some coins in the soda machine and said, "Well, this is the last time we'll be using this."

"Yeah, too bad," answered Phil. "Let's ask for one of these at the next student-council meeting."

"Not so fast!" It was Mrs. Garcia's booming voice coming from the doorway. All heads turned. The room instantly became dead quiet.

"I don't think this would be a good time for you to ask for anything," advised Mrs. Garcia. "When everyone finds out what you've done, you'll be lucky if they allow you to even eat in the cafeteria."

The students remained still while Mrs. Garcia looked eye-to-eye at each of them. "Don't feel like talking now, huh? I don't blame you. I sure wouldn't know what to say if I were in your shoes."

Bobby broke the silence. "Want a soda, Mrs. Garcia?" He offered her the can he was holding. No one laughed.

"This isn't a time for jokes, Bobby." Then she addressed everyone. "Okay, it's over now. It's time for you to think about what comes next. All the students are on their way home and will be telling their parents what happened today. Phone calls will be made, the principal and super-intendent will be told, and some people may even call the police. I don't think any of our school administrators will be happy. They know that parents will ask how school children could fool them so completely. Imagine how Mr. Alston will feel, and think about how he will react."

They continued to stare at her. Finally, Phil spoke up. "What should we do, Mrs. Garcia?"

Before she could respond, Gil jumped in. He wanted to show Mrs. Garcia that he had done some thinking about this. "Okay, it's over now. Let's think about what we're going to say to Mr. Alston." He then added, "Sorry I interrupted, Mrs. Garcia."

"That is the smartest thing I've heard you say so far," said Mrs. Garcia. "The way you handle yourselves from now on will have a lot to do with the way the principal responds."

Kelly said, "Why don't we just tell Mr. Alston and the teachers what we did and why we did it. Let's get it over with."

"Right," agreed Dusty. "We should tell him before anyone else does, and let's hope that he understands. Maybe he will be impressed that we ran the school so well and kids actually learned things."

"I think we're dead!" exclaimed Whitey. "Have any of you ever seen Stoney . . . sorry, Mrs. Garcia . . . give a compliment to a student? No! Do you think he will try to understand why we did this? No! He's going to be mad."

Gil spoke up. "He'll probably be really mad, but I don't think there's any other way out of this. He's going to find out anyway, and soon. It might as well be from us."

Mrs. Garcia said, "I think you're right, and the sooner the better. This can go one of two ways. It can be seen as quite an accomplishment, or it can be viewed as a terrible trick that put many students in danger. Also, it will be an embarrassment to the teachers. Mr. Alston has a better chance of seeing the good side of the situation if you handle yourselves well." She paused for a moment. "I think it would be best if I call Mr. Alston right now and tell him he is needed at the school immediately. When he gets here, you all do the explaining. Be respectful. Remember, when he walks in here, he will be absolutely shocked, and then he'll get angry."

Leo spoke up. "It could be pretty bad, I guess. We could even, like, get suspended or grounded for months. Maybe even get kicked out of school."

*** * *

All the students had worried looks on their faces. It was 3:15 P.M. Mrs. Garcia finished the conversation with, "I'll call Mr. Alston right now." She walked into the principal's office and shut the door. While Mrs. Garcia was gone, Leo whispered into Gil's ear. "Guess we have to tell her about the guy in the washroom, right?"

"Yes, I know," Gil responded. "We could get into even more trouble when they find out about him. They'll go crazy and say, 'See? Our children could have been hurt by that guy.'"

"But we can't just leave him there," said Leo.

"I know, but what are our choices?" Gil turned to the others and said, "Leo and I are trying to figure out what to do with the man in the washroom. You guys have any ideas?"

Phil said, "How about just untying him and letting him go?"

"No, no." answered Wes. "That'll make Stoney really mad."

Leo replied, "Our parents are going to flip out when they hear a burglar got into school. We'll totally be dead meat."

Dusty added, "Let's tell. They'll find out anyway. Since we want them to trust us, if they find out we didn't tell them, they'll never trust us again."

Whitey said, "Hey, maybe they'll call us heroes for capturing him."

"Oh, right!" said Phil.

Gil asked the next question. "Okay, but when do we tell her? Now, or when Stoney gets here?"

While the students were talking, Mrs. Garcia was explaining to the principal, "No, it's not the plumbing. It's another kind of emergency. Could you come over here right now?" She listened for a moment and answered, "It's about students. In fact, there are some fifth graders here right now. You'd better come over immediately." She hung up and returned to the students. "He's coming. Remember, everyone be honest."

"It's not that, Mrs. Garcia," Gil replied. "It . . . it's just that there's something else you don't know about."

"Uh oh." Mrs. Garcia said. "What is it, Gil?"

"Well, we had a visitor earlier today."

"Who?" Mrs. Garcia's voice was urgent.

"A guy from my neighborhood came into the hallway during lunch."

"Was he someone's parent?" asked the teacher.

"No!"

Mrs. Garcia frowned. "What happened? Tell me everything, Gil."

"Well, he tried to grab Donny Mueller, a kid in fourth grade."

"Oh no!" Mrs. Garcia almost shouted.

"He picked the wrong kid, though. Donny actually beat him up."

"What? How? Be serious with me."

Gil shifted from one leg to the other. "Uh . . . Donny said that he kicked him a good one where it hurts."

"Oh my goodness!" Mrs. Garcia shook her head like she was going to say, "What next?" Instead, she said, "I see. Did Donny get hurt?"

"No. He came running to us for help. We were all here in the teachers' lounge when it happened. Then he led us to the guy, who was lying on the floor of the boys' washroom near the fourth-grade rooms. We tied him to a pipe in the basement with duct tape. We didn't tell anyone because we didn't want to get discovered."

Mrs. Garcia immediately realized that all this had happened while she was reading magazines in the conference room. She quietly calmed herself knowing that Mr. Alston would be arriving soon. She continued in a controlled voice, "So, he's still in the basement?"

"Uh, no. Now he's tied up in the washroom. He got loose downstairs and tried to get away, but we nailed him again."

Mrs. Garcia asked sarcastically, "Another kick?"

"Naw, Dusty used the fire extinguisher on him this time. First he sprayed him, then he hit him with it in the gut."

"Dusty hit him?" Mrs. Garcia's turned her head toward him.

Dusty bent his arms up and pumped his fists back and forth to show his muscles. Mrs. Garcia ignored the gesture and asked, "Is the man hurt?"

Dusty spoke up. "No. He had a hard time seeing for a while, and he probably has a headache and a stomachache.

"Maybe he can untie himself again," said Mrs. Garcia. "You think?"

Gil said, "I don't think so. We wrapped him with a lot of duct tape."

"Hmm," she thought. "We'll tell Mr. Alston about him when he gets here. He'll know what to do. You all have certainly had a remarkable day, haven't you? It's actually all hard to believe."

* * *

Mr. Alston's eyebrows jumped halfway up his forehead when he walked into the teachers' lounge and saw the group of fifth-grade students. He was wearing blue jeans and a turtleneck sweater. Mrs. Garcia was seated at one of the tables with the students. Her face was calm but serious. Mr. Alston looked confused.

"Mrs. Garcia, what are these students doing here, and how did they get into my school?"

Mrs. Garcia said, "Mr. Alston, the students have something to tell you." She pointed to the group.

Mr. Alston kept his gaze on Mrs. Garcia a moment longer, then turned toward the stunned-looking group of students. Gil broke the silence. "There was never a plumbing problem, Mr. Alston."

Eyebrows bounced. "What?" The principal shouted. He glanced at Mrs. Garcia, then back at Gil.

"We set it up to look like a plumbing problem so we could keep you and the teachers away from school, just for today."

"But . . . I got a call from the water department."

"The call wasn't from the water department. It was from a friend of mine. It wasn't just us in the school today either. The whole school was here—all the students."

Mr. Alston was stunned. "That can't be! No one was here."

"Well, we were here, and we had a regular school day with every class."

"No! This can't be!" he repeated.

"It's true, Mr. Alston, and it worked. Most of us taught classes, and the students learned."

Mr. Alston looked from Gil to the students to Mrs. Garcia. It took him some time to think about what he was hearing.

Gil continued, "We didn't mean any disrespect. We just wanted to show you that we don't like to be treated like babies. We wanted to show you that we can do a good job on things and be responsible."

Mr. Alston interrupted. "You think we are treating you like babies? Keep in mind that you are only ten years old."

Gil went on. "Remember when PeeWee Reese got knocked down at recess last week?" Mr. Alston nodded his head. "Well, we felt that punishing all of us for what one person did wasn't fair. You said that you didn't like us playing Catch One–Catch All—that it made everyone hyper. Well, when PeeWee got hurt, that was the only time anyone ever got hurt from that game, and only one person knocked PeeWee down, not all of us."

Mr. Alston said, "And you thought coming into school like this would prove to me that you can do a good job . . . by running the school?"

"Well, . . . yes!"

Gil told about the meeting at Cameron Field. He explained how students observed other classes to see what was being taught so they knew what to do.

"I'm flabbergasted!" he said. "How did you get into the building?"

When Gil answered, Mr. Alston raised one eyebrow and said, "Well, we'll have that window taken care of immediately."

"We weren't trying to show you up or anything, Mr. Alston. We just wanted to show you we are mature enough to handle a tough job."

The principal laughed sarcastically. "Ha! Weren't trying to show me up, huh?" Then he turned to Mrs. Garcia. "Cindy, were you in on this?"

"No, I didn't know anything about it. I discovered what was happening when I came to school to get my wallet earlier today," replied Mrs. Garcia. "They were so sincere, Mr. Alston. I saw that the school was operating very well. Everyone was well-behaved. It was like a normal day at school. I decided to let them proceed. I stayed in the school to keep an eye on things for the rest of the afternoon and to be available if an emergency arose. Believe me, if anything had gone wrong, I would have stepped in right away and taken over, and that includes calling you immediately."

While Gil and Mrs. Garcia were explaining things to Mr. Alston, Sarah happened to see the photocopy of Priscilla's hand hanging from the teachers' bulletin board. She thought that might not look like what "responsible" students would do. When she saw that Mr. Alston was focused on Mrs. Garcia and the other students, Sarah casually got up from her table and walked toward the sink to get a drink. She kept her eyes on Mr. Alston as she quickly snatched the photo from under a thumbtack on the bulletin board. She pressed the paper against her hip and dropped it into the trash. Priscilla watched her as she returned to her chair. When their eyes met, Priscilla flashed a quick smile and mouthed the words, "Thank you." Sarah nodded.

"So there was school all day today for everyone?"

"Yes, Sir," said Gil.

"Do the parents know?"

"Not yet," answered Gil. "When we planned this we didn't think about their reactions."

"Oh my goodness, you didn't think about their reactions?" Mr. Alston repeated.

"There's one more thing we have to tell you, Mr. Alston." Gil looked uneasy, like when you have to tell your parents something bad.

The same eyebrow jumped. "More surprises, Gil? Not sure I can take another one. What is it this time?"

"Some guy snuck into school at lunchtime. He wasn't very nice, so we've got him tied up in the fourth-grade boys' washroom."

"What? In the washroom? Is he still there?"

"Uh-huh."

"Some guy? An adult or a young person?"

"Adult."

"What did you tie him up with?"

"Suspenders and duct tape!"

Mr. Alston looked over at Dusty quickly, then turned to Mrs. Garcia. "Did you know about this too?"

She said, "They told me right after I called you, about fifteen minutes ago."

Mr. Alston then asked Gil, "How did you manage to tie him up?"

"We doused him with fire extinguisher stuff, and Dusty hit him with the tank."

"Dusty Rhodes?" Mr. Alston looked again at Dusty. Dusty smiled and gave a small wave.

"Did he hurt you, Dusty?"

"No."

"Did he hurt anyone?"

"No," said Gil. Wes thought it would be better if he said nothing about the man grabbing him during his escape.

"All right!" Mr. Alston said. It sounded like he was finished with the questions and was ready to retake the school. "Mrs. Garcia, you come with me. I want the rest of you to sit in here while Mrs. Garcia and I tend to the visitor in the washroom." He waved a finger at the students. "Don't leave yet. I'm not finished talking to you."

He led Mrs. Garcia toward the washroom. "Let's take a look and see what we've got in here." He opened the washroom door and saw a man sitting on the floor. Most of the man's arms were covered in tape. The two men looked at each other but neither spoke. Mr. Alston ducked back into the hallway. "It definitely looks like that man has had a rough day. I have to call the police."

They hurried to the office. After making the call, he said, "The police will be here shortly. Cindy, I can't believe what has happened here today. I have got to think about what we do now. You and I both know the parents and the rest of the people in this town are going to wonder how all of this could happen. We could all be fired."

The Envelope

"I'm going to look like a fool when the parents and the community find out. This could very well be the end of my career. A school board won't trust a principal who was tricked by students to stay home while they ran the school." He pulled out a handkerchief and wiped his face.

Mrs. Garcia said, "Well, maybe it isn't so bad, Walter. How about explaining it in a positive way? Rather than saying they fooled us, let's talk about how well-organized they were and how carefully they planned everything. We have been telling the parents how we've been teaching children to think for themselves and work on their problem-solving skills. This is a good example of that. They took a problem and came up with an idea they thought was good. Of course, we don't necessarily think it was a good idea. However, they could have sulked or become discipline problems. Instead, they organized and planned with intelligence, and fortunately it worked. When you think about it, it's quite impressive, even if they did go way too far." She looked at him and smiled.

"Impressive, all right, but we still look like idiots," he answered.

"Okay," she agreed. "They fooled us, and this was a big one, but this isn't the first time kids put something over on their teachers. I say we admit to the parents that we were fooled, and we'll learn from it. The truth would come out anyway; there are 250 witnesses. If we try to talk our way out of it, we won't look very good. Instead, we tell the community that we will assure them that a situation like this will never happen again. That's the way to present our explanation in a positive way.

"Walter, you are the perfect man for this. You will be terrific telling everyone that this experience shows that our kids are special. They worked hard and acted responsibly on a project they created. They showed good planning and problem-solving skills. They worked out the hundreds of small problems that arise every day for us teachers. They did something they shouldn't have, but they sure did it well."

* * *

Dusty looked up at the teachers' lounge clock. "It's 3:40 already. I hope they hurry up in there. My mom gets worried when I'm not home on time."

The students could hear the office phone ringing. Dusty knew it would be parents calling to talk to the principal. He said, "I'm glad I don't have to answer that phone anymore. It looks like Stoney isn't answering it either."

Mr. Alston suddenly walked into the lounge, and all heads turned to face him. He was holding a letter in his hand. Mrs. Garcia was following behind, holding a small stack of papers that had the school heading at the top. Mr. Alston spoke in his official tone.

"I am very upset that you tricked us all with your little project today. I am troubled when I think of all the things that could have gone wrong, especially regarding the safety of every child in this school. He paused, then added, "I am impressed, however, by how well you conducted yourselves. You handled your individual jobs well from what I understand. That takes hard work, but it also takes thoughtfulness and caring. That is especially true in a school that has really small children."

He raised the paper he was holding in his hand. "I want you to take this letter home and come back to school tonight with your parents. Here's what it says.

Dear Parents,

We had a very unusual and special experience at school today. It is so unusual, however, that a letter cannot come close to giving a proper explanation.

I find it necessary to call for an emergency meeting of parents, teachers, and administrators tonight. Please join me at seven o'clock in our school auditorium with your children if you so choose. It is important that you know everything that has occurred. I apologize for the late notice, but it couldn't be avoided. I hope to see you later.

Sincerely,
Mr. Alston
Central School Principal

Mrs. Garcia handed out copies of the letter to all the students. Mr. Alston said, "Go straight home now. It's late. No stopping at a friend's house. Your families are probably worried about you. And tell your parents to call their friends about tonight's meeting. Okay, go."

The students filed out of the teachers' lounge and left the school. Mrs. Garcia looked proud of them. The principal wiped his face again. The two grown-ups walked together to the entrance to watch their students leave in different directions. Mr. Alston spoke. "They sure are an unusual bunch of kids, aren't they?"

"Uh-huh."

"I have to call the superintendent now, Cindy. I'm not looking forward to that phone call."

"She's a reasonable person, Walter. She knows you're a good leader. Stay positive, and remember that you are respected by the people of this community. You will do an excellent job tonight. You always do." She squeezed his hand and began walking away. "See you at seven."

"Thanks, Cindy. See you later." He smiled as she left, trying to build up the same confidence she had.

Two police cars pulled up to the school as Mrs. Garcia drove away. Pete Larkin and another officer ran up to the entrance. "Where is he, Walter?"

"Hello, Pete. He's in the boys' washroom right around the corner there."

* * *

Word spread quickly about the takeover. Every parent who had a child at the school got the news one way or another, and the entire community was buzzing about it by dinnertime.

At 6:50 P.M., Mr. Winter, the custodian, placed a microphone at the center of the auditorium stage. He twisted its neck back and forth to raise the mike up to his mouth. The large room was filling with students and parents. Most of the teachers were there also, sitting together at the back of the auditorium. Gil, Becky, and their parents sat with the Rhodes family in the fourth row. Becky sat on Gil's lap. She reached over and gently pulled down the top of Dusty's ear, then let it snap back. The boys laughed. Dusty said, "Easy, Becky." He took her hand and shook it. She laughed and shook his hand too.

Each boy knew that the other had survived his after-school talk at home. Gil told his parents what this meeting was going to be about. Both his parents were angry when they heard about the takeover. "What on earth were you thinking?" asked Gil's father. "Do you have any idea of the harm you could have brought to those students, not to mention yourself?" He ranted for ten minutes while Gil sat and listened.

They had phoned Dusty's parents and had that can-you-believe-this conversation. The Rhodeses were calm but serious. Mrs. Rhodes said, "We were very surprised to hear what they did, Sharon. Dusty is being very quiet. We're going to listen to what Mr. Alston has to say before coming to any conclusions. How's Gil?"

"Well, after he told us what happened, he was also quiet, but at the same time he almost seems proud of what they did. This isn't like him. I never would have guessed our two guys could do anything like this."

Mr. and Mrs. Hodges calmed down after that phone conversation. They decided to follow the Rhodes' idea and wait to hear what Mr. Alston had to say.

At exactly seven o'clock, Mr. Alston walked up onto the stage. He spotted his boss, the superintendent of schools, sitting in the back row talking with parents. He nodded to her, and she nodded back. He looked nervous as he wrestled the microphone up to his own height. The audience could hear his breathing through the speakers. The room quieted as he stood up straighter and cleared his throat.

"Good evening, ladies and gentlemen. Thank you for coming here tonight on such short notice. Today, as you know by now, many of our fifth-grade students executed the most astonishing and disturbing exercise in our school's fifty-five-year history. They figured out a way to keep my staff and me out of school today. Then they conducted a normal school day with our students—without us! It is quite incredible, I must admit.

"That means they taught every grade and all special classes from 8:50 A.M. until 3:00 P.M. this afternoon.

From what I've been told by some students, all classrooms were conducted on their regular schedules. I was told that that there were very good learning experiences during the day. In addition, there were students serving as playground supervisors, nurse, custodian, secretary, the milk-line supervisor, and even principal.

He hesitated here, and slowly looked up to his audience with a slight smile on his face. There was polite laughter from the parents. He continued, "Perhaps you have heard some of the details before coming here tonight."

"That is the good news. The bad news is that what they did could be considered dishonest, dangerous, and even illegal. Our children's safety was put in jeopardy. Many different situations arose here today, just as they do in the course of a normal school day. Some difficult situations arose that could have led to unfortunate results. Most were minor, but some were dangerous. Our kids handled them well, so I'm told. I still find it upsetting and will learn about the details in the coming days. However, it is all over now with no negative results as far as I know. I will inform you of those unusual activities in the coming days.

"I have been considering what to do about this extraordinary situation, and every time I think of a punishment, it is matched by the good work these fifth-graders did. I am also considering the reasons they gave for their actions.

"A number of fifth-grade students felt that during this school year they were being treated unfairly because of the poor behavior of a few. Their purpose in today's exercise was to illustrate to me that they can be responsible enough to handle tough jobs."

He raised his eyes from his notes to face the audience. "They have convinced me of that. It is not easy to run a school, even for one day—believe me! To be honest, I would never have thought that the children were capable of doing what they did today. They proved me wrong."

Mrs. Dower was sitting among the other teachers. She looked angry as she listened to the principal.

Mr. Alston continued. "So, at our next student-council meeting, I will listen more closely to the students' issues and ideas about school policy. However, tonight I have two promises to present to you. First, I will take a closer look at our attitudes about our students' abilities to handle higher responsibilities; and second, I assure you that this school will provide the safest possible learning environment for every single student. The kind of situation that happened here today, or anything like it, will never be repeated.

"In return, I want a promise from the students that they will not plan any more surprises like what we had today. I expect that all ideas and complaints will be aired at student-council meetings or in my office, and I promise that I will listen to them thoughtfully and consider their ideas and suggestions."

He paused again, sounding even more serious. "What happened today was completely inappropriate. What these students did was a serious breach of trust.

I do not support what has happened, and frankly, I am embarrassed that it occurred. I understand why they did it, however, and I realize, also, that these students achieved something very special, and it was for a worthy purpose.

"At this point I would like to open the meeting for questions. I am sure you have many. All known facts will be told." Suddenly he pointed to Gil, Dusty, Kelly, and Sadie to join him on the stage and said, "These students and Mrs. Garcia will assist me in answering your questions."

The four students gathered together on the stage. They stood shoulder to shoulder. There were plenty of questions.

"How did you get such a wild idea?"

"Did anyone get hurt?"

"There must have been some students who were nervous that no grownups were there. How did you handle them?"

"There must have been visitors at the school during the day who would see that no adults were there? How did you get away with that?"

"Who organized all this?"

"I am quite amazed that the kids could keep it together for the whole day."

"Weren't there discipline problems that needed to be handled? How did that go?

The questions and comments came fast and furious. The four students described actual learning activities and events and appeared to be enjoying their time on stage. Mr. Alston and Mrs. Garcia answered other questions rather nervously.

One of the parents said, "I'm not so sure a fifth-grade student can adequately "teach" anything to another grade-school student."

Sadie jumped right in with her response. "Well, we had a very good lesson on proper punctuation of sentences. We covered periods, commas, apostrophes, and quotation marks." Some of the moms and dads nodded their heads like they were impressed.

Kelly added, "We discussed sound waves in our science period. Kristen Hunt demonstrated how a drinking straw made a higher pitch when the sound traveled over a shorter distance. The audience responded with some quiet "Mmms" and other comments. Kelly continued, "She actually played the entire musical scale on a straw." That brought a bunch of smiles, and a few people clapped.

"That's all fine," snapped one bothered parent, "but I want to know that my child is safe at school. I want to know that there is an adult there whom I feel will take good care of our children if there's an accident or emergency."

Mr. Alston replied, "Well, I do see your point. Of course I agree that our teachers and staff are better equipped to handle emergencies than our children are. They did have a few bumps and scratches during the day, but these kids did a fantastic job of helping those in need. You can be sure that we will be dealing most seriously with the safety issue.

After an hour of questions and answers, people began drifting out of the auditorium one family at a time. When the superintendent stood up to leave, she gave the thumbs up sign to Mr. Alston. Mrs. Garcia noticed he smiled back at her. It looked like she and her boss were not going to be fired after all. Mr. Alston thanked everyone again for coming and ended the meeting.

In the crowded hallway outside the auditorium Mr. and Mrs. Stanky, Eddie's parents, were patting Priscilla on the back and thanking her for helping their son. Eddie's mom asked what happened to the pants and socks. Priscilla responded, "Oh, I forgot. They're in the class bathroom in the garbage can." Mr. Stanky smiled and said to his wife, "I'll get them, Hon."

"In another corner, Mr. and Mrs. Mueller were shaking Sadie's hand. "Thanks for helping Donny when he was upset. He doesn't like surprises, but somehow you got him through the day. He came home feeling very proud of himself this afternoon."

As they inched out of the auditorium, Gil was looking over the crowd. He suddenly peeled off from his parents, "I'll be right back," he said, and weaved his way through families to say hello to the Lockmans.

"Hi, Mr. and Mrs. Lockman! Hi, Whitey!"

"Hello, Gil," said Mrs. Lockman. "You all certainly fooled a lot of people today."

Mr. Lockman took Gil's hand and said, "I have to shake your hand, Gil. You've done something I've tried to do for the last four years."

Mrs. Lockman displayed a puzzled look at her husband and said, "What's that, Dear?"

"Oh nothing, Malia. It's just that Gil showed excellent leadership today." He turned to Gil and said, "You know, I was right about you. You are a very special guy to organize something like this. In fact, I have something to give you that expresses my feelings." Mr. Lockman handed Gil a small envelope. Gil quickly stuffed it into his front pocket.

"Thanks, Mr. Lockman."

"You are very welcome, Gil."

Whitey said. "Hey, what's in the envelope?"

Mr. Lockman answered, "Oh, just a little something I promised Gil a while back. It's no big deal. Let's go home."

As Priscilla walked toward the door with her parents she suddenly squealed, "*Oooh*, there's Sarah!" She dragged her parents by their hands toward Sarah and Mrs. Glum. They met near the exit door.

"Mom, Dad, this is Sarah."

They turned to Mrs. Glum and Sarah and introduced themselves with smiles and handshakes. Mr. Wright said, "It's nice to meet you, Sarah. Priscilla told us that you helped her out today. She said you are cool under pressure." He then turned to Sarah's mom. "You've got a gem of a daughter there, Mrs. Glum. Priscilla told us how Sarah took over during an awkward situation and helped Priscilla get through it."

Mrs. Glum beamed a happy smile. "It's very nice to meet you. How nice of you to say that! I see that Sarah has talents I haven't yet discovered."

Mrs. Wright said, "Hey, how about coming over tomorrow night for dinner. We're just having hamburgers and hot dogs, but we'd love to have you."

Sarah looked at her mother.

"Yes, we'd love to come. I'll bring a salad. Is that all right?"

"Perfect. How about six o'clock?"

"Six it is," said Mrs. Glum.

Sarah and Priscilla exchanged huge smiles.

* * *

At 8:45 P.M., Mrs. Garcia said goodnight to the last family, and stood with Mr. Alston as he locked the door behind them. Everyone had gone. The night was suddenly very quiet as they stood at the door. "It went pretty well, didn't it?" she asked.

"Better than I expected, Cindy. I thought it would have been a lot worse."

"You were wonderful, Walter. You explained exactly what happened, and they respected you for that. You are a very good principal, and I am proud to work with you."

"Thank you, Cindy. You have been very helpful through all of this, but it isn't over yet. The news will spread like wildfire through the community and around the state. We'll just have to continue to be straight with them and hope for the best."

"Exactly," she said. As they walked to their cars, Mrs. Garcia added, "I would love to have heard the conversations between a few of these kids and their parents. I'm sure there were a lot of shocked moms and dads in town tonight."

"Count me in as one of them!" he answered.

Two cars suddenly arrived at curbside and squealed to a stop near them. Three men and two women rushed out of their cars. They were holding writing pads, a camera, and minirecorders. A woman said, "Excuse me. Are you Mr. Alston, the principal of this school?"

Mr. Alston looked sideways at Mrs. Garcia and said in a low voice, "Well, here we go!"

Mrs. Garcia scooted away to her car.

The News

The Saturday morning newspaper headline read:

STUDENTS TAKE OVER SCHOOL
FIFTH GRADERS AT CENTRAL SCHOOL CONDUCT CLASSES ALL DAY FRIDAY, OVERPOWER INTRUDER

There was a caption underneath a photo of Mr. Alston.

Mr. Walter Alston, Central School principal, said, "I was told there was a plumbing problem, and I fell for it. We've had water main breaks before."

At the bottom of the page was a picture of Leo holding up a first-aid book. The caption read, *Central's acting nurse for the day was fifth-grader Leo Durocher.*

The article continued on page two with a picture of Donny glaring at the camera like an angry rock star. The caption read, *Donald Mueller, fourth grader, used a plunger to help overpower an intruder.*

Dusty called Gil early Saturday morning and asked, "Did you see the paper?"

"I did!"

"Did Leo take that first-aid book home with him?" asked Dusty.

"I don't know. Did you see Donny's picture?

"Yes! He's the most famous kid in the school now," answered Dusty. "Man, last night there were news guys outside our house until midnight. My parents slammed the front door on them around ten-thirty. I never heard so many questions in my life. Did you have reporters at your house?"

"Oh, only about 100."

"How'd they find out so fast?"

Gil said, "I don't know. I'll bet one of the parents called. Oh, they took my picture standing between my parents. Did they take yours?"

Dusty was excited. "Yep, a lot, and there were TV cameras too. There's nothing on TV yet, though. My dad told me to stay inside this morning. He said the news people would probably be back today."

"I know," answered Gil. "Hey, want to come over later?"

"Okay! I'll ask my mom."

* * *

The night before, around the time the school meeting was ending, the newspaper got an anonymous phone call. A man said that Central School had been run by students all day Friday. The newspaper called the police department to check. "Yes, we know about it," said the sergeant. "We got a call from the principal around three thirty. You'd better talk to him about what happened. We have no comment at this time."

The principal faced the camera and recorders that were held in front of him. "Yes, that's right. We had a meeting with the parents about it that lasted until just a few minutes ago. I'll tell you what happened." He gave a brief description of the day, starting with the phone call he got on Thursday night. He said that lessons were taught in every classroom by fifth-grade students. The reporters yelled over each other, trying to ask their questions. Mr. Alston raised his hands and said he was very tired, it had been a long day, and he needed to go home. He told them the superintendent's office would issue a formal announcement in the morning. He walked to his car as they yelled more questions. He ignored them, climbed into his car, and waved a polite good-bye as he drove off.

The TV news aired the story on Saturday morning. Donny was the first to appear on the screen. "The guy grabbed me by the shirt and flung me across the floor." He waved his arms to help describe the toss. "When he came at me, I ran into the boys' washroom."

"Were you scared?" asked a reporter.

"Yeah, I was real scared!" he answered. "He followed me in and told me to keep quiet. That's when I grabbed the plunger and smacked him . . . right on the head!" He clasped his hands together and swung an imaginary plunger. "When he grabbed his head, I kicked him hard . . . you know where."

A reporter appeared on screen and told more of Donny's story. He called him a hero. "There's no telling what

Mr. Thompson might have done if Donny hadn't stopped him in that washroom."

The superintendent appeared on the TV screen. She gave a boring speech about how wonderful the teachers at Central School are and how lucky they were to have Mr. Alston as principal. Then she told the parents that steps had already been taken to ensure that nothing like this would ever happen again in their school system. She finished by saying, "On the twenty-sixth of this month, we will have our next board of education meeting. Changes will be announced about what the school district will do to prevent another occurrence like this.

Gil and Dusty were the last TV interviews shown. Gil looked directly into the camera and said, "We were trying to show that we could do something good."

Dusty, with thumbs hooked under his suspenders, added, "I covered the office with Gil, and Leo was the nurse."

Gil ended with, "I'll be glad when we go back to school Monday morning with our real teachers."

EPILOGUE

Five weeks later, on a chilly Friday afternoon, five kids were standing around, talking near the flagpole. "Well, it's been over a month now. Doesn't it seem like a lot longer?" said Priscilla.

"Yeah," said Whitey. "I guess it all turned out all right. None of us got into any big trouble."

Dusty said, "Actually, we pretty much got what we wanted. Stoney listens to us at student council meetings now . . . for the first time ever."

"At least he's trying," said Sadie. "It's a little weird seeing him stand by the front door when we leave school every day. I like how he waves his arms, saying 'bye-bye' and gives high fives."

Whitey suddenly began flipping his eyebrows. "Goodbye now, everybody. Go straight home! Be nice to your parents, and do your homework!"

They all laughed. "You're good at that, Whitey," chuckled Kelly.

Whitey added, "Even my dad is beginning to like him. Remember when he stood up at the end of that meeting with the police chief and the state guy? I couldn't believe it when my dad actually complimented Stoney on the way he handled our protests."

* * *

A special meeting had been held three weeks after "Takeover Friday," as the students called it. It began sharply at seven o'clock in the evening.

"Good evening, everyone. My name is Wilma Rudolph. As a member of the board of education I am chairing this meeting. Sitting next to me are Assistant Chief of Police Roberto Clemente; to his left is Bob Gibson, representing the state superintendent's office; and on my right is Mr. Walter Alston, principal of Central School. I see that there are lots of students and parents here tonight, so let's begin the proceedings.

"This is the first of four probation meetings to be held in this auditorium according to the board's ruling. Our purpose is to keep track of the behavior and attitude of the students involved in the illegal entry of Central School last month. We will continue to meet at three-month intervals for one year, as required by the ruling. If, at any time our panel decides that the students involved have not maintained the status of good citizens, we will exercise our right to suspend them from school as directed by the board of education."

Mrs. Rudolph glanced toward the principal and said, "First to speak tonight will be Mr. Alston, who will update us on student behavior and student-council progress. Assistant Chief Clemente will follow with questions to Mr. Alston and the students regarding behavior. Finally, there will be a three-minute per person open microphone opportunity for anyone in the audience who would like to address this panel with comments or questions." She turned toward the principal and said, "Mr. Alston."

* * *

Dusty leaned against the flagpole and agreed with Whitey about his dad. "He was the only one in the audience that night who said anything. He was cool. Even Mrs. Rudolph complimented him on his kind words about Mr. Alston."

Sarah Glum suddenly came out of school and walked by the group as they were talking. She waved as she walked by. "Hey, Sarah. C'mon over," yelled Sadie. "We're talking about the big 'special' meeting."

"Can't!" she answered. "Priscilla's family is coming over for dinner. I have to get home and help get ready." She waved again and walked on.

"Let's go, Gil," said Dusty. "We'd better get home."

Everyone said good-bye. On their way home Dusty talked about the science experiments they were working on. Suddenly Hank pulled up to the curb beside them on his motorcycle. He was smiling.

"Hi, guys. How you doing?"

"Good, Hank. Haven't seen you lately," said Gil.

"I've been busy doing the community service that the judge ordered.

Dusty said, "Oh yeah, over at the nursing home, right?"

"And I'm just getting home from my new job at Joe's Motor Repair Center over in Milburn. Joe is a really good guy, and smart too. He knows everything about motors."

"Oh yeah, and guess what else!" Hank said with an excited voice. "On Monday I begin my mechanics course. It will only take six months to finish. If I pass, which I know I will, I'll be a certified motorcycle mechanic."

"Cool," said Dusty. Gil smiled.

Hank added, "Funny how it all turned out. I could be in jail right now. Instead, I'm able to go to school, and after that I begin my mechanic's career. All thanks to you, Gil. You actually turned my life around. I'm the luckiest guy in the world."

Both boys smiled. "Hey, any time either of you guys want to take a ride on my bike, just let me know."

"Wow! Okay, Hank. Thanks!"

"All right, I gotta go," said Hank. "See you around." He put his cycle in gear and roared off down the road.

"Gil, think you'll ever get that $1,000 back?"

"Sure, Dusty. He'll keep his word, and he needs the money a lot more than I do right now. I told him no hurry, I won't need it until I go to college." They continued their walk.

Dusty asked, "Think Mrs. Dower will ever change?"

"Are you kidding? Since all this happened her hair has gotten tighter and she's starting to gray. There's no hope for her, Dusty."

"Well, Stoney sure has changed," Dusty replied. At least we got one grumpy person to be better. There's always hope."

"Yeah, I guess so, but I think Mrs. Dower is beyond hope."

Suddenly Gil's dad tooted his horn and waved from his car as he passed by. "Your dad's home early today," said Dusty.

"Yeah, we're going out to dinner tonight. My mom and dad told me they decided we should spend more family fun time together. My dad said something about enjoying his children before they're gone."

Dusty snapped a suspender. "Cool!"

ABOUT THE AUTHOR

Jack Spangenberger grew up in South Orange, NJ. He graduated from Our Lady of Sorrows grammar school and Columbia High School. He has a BS from Fairleigh Dickinson University, Madison, NJ, and an MAT from Northwestern University, Evanston, IL. He taught grade school for thirty-one years in Wilmette, IL. Jack has two sons, Eric and Jeff, that he raised with his former wife, Sandy, in Northbrook, IL. He lives with his wife, Sharon, in Chicago, IL.

Takeover is Jack's first book of fiction.

Made in the USA
Columbia, SC
05 March 2018